"I Am Choosing This Of My Free Will, Father,"

Caitlyn told the priest.

"As am I," Grant said so convincingly that Caitlyn found herself wishing he really meant it. That her husband truly wanted her to be his wife in every respect, and not just the "bonus" her father had promised his foreman.

Her husband!

As much as she would have liked to indulge such fantasies, Caitlyn refused to delude herself. Love played no part in this travesty of a vow. Why, her father might just as well have sold her off to the highest bidder!

Father O'Reilly beamed at Grant. "You may now kiss the bride."

Grant placed a light kiss upon her lips. Considering the circumstances, his tenderness was so unexpected, it made her knees buckle. Her heart gave a hopeful leap. Perhaps this marriage would continue to surprise her happily....

Dear Reader,

Please join us in celebrating Silhouette's 20th anniversary in 2000! We promise to deliver—all year—passionate, powerful, provocative love stories from your favorite Desire authors!

This January, look for bestselling author Leanne Banks's first MAN OF THE MONTH with *Her Forever Man.* Watch sparks fly when irresistibly rugged ranch owner Brock Logan comes face-to-face with his new partner, the fiery Felicity Chambeau, in the first book of Leanne's brand-new miniseries LONE STAR FAMILIES: THE LOGANS.

Desire is pleased to continue the Silhouette cross-line continuity ROYALLY WED with *The Pregnant Princess* by favorite author Anne Marie Winston. After a night of torrid passion with a stranger, a beautiful princess ends up pregnant…and seeks out the father of her child.

Elizabeth Bevarly returns to Desire with her immensely popular miniseries FROM HERE TO MATERNITY with *Dr. Mommy,* about a couple reunited by a baby left on a doorstep. *Hard Lovin' Man,* another of Peggy Moreland's TEXAS BRIDES, captures the intensity of falling in love when a cowgirl gives her heart to a sweet-talkin', hard-lovin' hunk. Cathleen Galitz delivers a compelling marriage-of-convenience tale in *The Cowboy Takes a Bride,* in the series THE BRIDAL BID. And Sheri WhiteFeather offers another provocative Native American hero in *Skyler Hawk: Lone Brave.*

Help us celebrate 20 years of great romantic fiction from Silhouette by indulging yourself with all six delectably sensual Desire titles each and every month during this special year!

Enjoy!

Joan Marlow Golan
Senior Editor, Silhouette Desire

Please address questions and book requests to:
Silhouette Reader Service
U.S.: 3010 Walden Ave., P.O. Box 1325, Buffalo, NY 14269
Canadian: P.O. Box 609, Fort Erie, Ont. L2A 5X3

The Cowboy Takes a Bride

CATHLEEN GALITZ

Published by Silhouette Books
America's Publisher of Contemporary Romance

To my loving father, Cecil Connors,
whose livelihood depended on the oil field for
many years. Thank you for acting as my trusted
adviser on this book—and in my life.

 SILHOUETTE BOOKS

ISBN 0-373-76271-2

THE COWBOY TAKES A BRIDE

Copyright © 2000 by Cathleen Galitz

All rights reserved. Except for use in any review, the reproduction
or utilization of this work in whole or in part in any form by any
electronic, mechanical or other means, now known or hereafter
invented, including xerography, photocopying and recording, or in
any information storage or retrieval system, is forbidden without
the written permission of the editorial office, Silhouette Books,
300 East 42nd Street, New York, NY 10017 U.S.A.

All characters in this book have no existence outside the imagination of
the author and have no relation whatsoever to anyone bearing the same
name or names. They are not even distantly inspired by any individual
known or unknown to the author, and all incidents are pure invention.

This edition published by arrangement with Harlequin Books S.A.

® and TM are trademarks of Harlequin Books S.A., used under license.
Trademarks indicated with ® are registered in the United States Patent
and Trademark Office, the Canadian Trade Marks Office and in other
countries.

Visit us at www.romance.net

Printed in U.S.A.

CATHLEEN GALITZ,

a Wyoming native, teaches English to seventh to twelfth graders in a rural school that houses kindergartners and seniors in the same building. She lives in a small Wyoming town with her husband and two children. When she's not busy writing, teaching or working with her Cub Scout den, she can most often be found hiking or snowmobiling in the Wind River Mountains.

IT'S OUR 20th ANNIVERSARY!
We'll be celebrating all year, starting with these fabulous titles, on sale in January 2000.

One

"**N**ow what?" Grant asked, wiping the sweat from his forehead with the back of his hand.

Behind him, Copper Mountain rose from the plains like a great dark whale breaching against a cerulean sky. Before him, the sage-covered desert stretched into the distance where a trail of dust heralded the arrival of an unannounced visitor to the oil rig. It was not a welcome sight.

The day was ungodly hot, he was already tired and out of sorts, and the last thing he needed right about now was another interruption. Earlier in the day he'd discovered the drilling line was as frayed and worn as the shoestring on which they were operating, and he'd had to re-spool a new one. On an already tight schedule, the process cost time he could ill afford. To top it all off, an hour ago the driller had stumbled out of the bunkhouse reeking of alcohol. The owner offered to take over the key position himself, but at fifty-eight Paddy Flynn was no longer a young man, and both the rigors of the oil field and the unreasonable demands he'd made upon his body left him in no shape to perform such strenuous duties.

Unwilling to put his employees' lives and limbs in the irresponsible hands of a drunken driller, Grant had no other choice but to fire the man on the spot and assume the job himself. A troubleshooter, he rotated between all of L.L. Drilling's operations. Mentally Grant corrected himself. *What was left of L.L. Drilling's operations.*

Everyone knew that this rig was the company's last hope for staying solvent. To put it in Paddy's own words, if they didn't hit a deep pocket soon, they'd all be *plumb bust.*

The 1990s hadn't been kind to the oil industry. Just to keep afloat, they'd been forced to sell off all but two of their big rigs and had kept only a handful of work-overs for service jobs. With each sale, Grant saw his dream of someday buying a ranch slipping away. He already had the place picked out. It was a prime piece of unspoiled Wyoming wilderness, tucked away on the side of a mountain. If he closed his eyes he could almost see it, could almost hear the trill of the river that threaded its way snakelike through a meadow big enough to hold and capture a man's heart.

At the sound of the vehicle coming to a stop below, Grant forced his eyes open. Trouble never bothered sneaking up on him. He groaned at the sight of the passenger who climbed out from behind the steering wheel in the dirt parking lot below. The absolute last thing he needed right about now was for some hot little number in tight jeans and a T-shirt to step out of her brand-new four-wheel drive and distract an already unruly crew. From their reaction to the news that good old Harry had just been run off, Grant knew they were disappointed to hear that their drinking buddy had just been replaced by the company hard-ass. Even under the best of circumstances it was bound to take a couple of shifts with no complications just to get his men in synch.

"Hey babe—y!" someone hollered down as the woman opened the door and took her first step into the blinding sunlight.

The vehicle shook slightly as she slammed the door shut behind her. A fine layer of dust sifted to the ground like a sprinkling of brown sugar. The hint of shiny, fire-engine red paint peeking out from beneath the remaining layers of grime indicated to Grant that the woman must be a greenhorn. It was unlikely a Wyoming native would take a new vehicle on the kind of back roads that led to this rig. The driver had to either be lost, crazy, or so filthy rich that she didn't have to worry about scraping together money for costly repairs. None of the possibilities endeared her any to Grant.

Even from a distance he could see that she was striking. The sun glinted off a mass of glossy, dark mahogany hair that hung below her shoulders. Always a sucker for a pretty brunette, Grant felt something inside him stir at the sight of her squinting up in the general vicinity from which a low wolfish whistle emanated.

Jamming his hard hat back on his head, he swore softly. Though he didn't condone such chauvinistic behavior, he hoped the men's catcalls might just scare the lost little lamb off before she stepped into the midst of this pack of wolves. What with the overtime they'd been putting in, most of the crew hadn't even seen a woman for better than a month, let alone one who looked like she'd stepped out of the pages of some slick movie magazine. Maybe that actually was where he'd seen her before. For some reason she looked familiar.

Grant knew that coming between a crew of horny men and the sexiest thing they were likely to see in another month of long Sundays wasn't going to improve his popularity any. It was just lucky for her that popularity wasn't a prerequisite for being a decent man.

Over the years Grant had earned more than his fair share of battle scars protecting a lady's honor. To be honest some were no more than pathetic barflies, but at least he usually had the privilege of getting to know them prior to scuffling over their questionable virtue.

Unfortunately rather than doing the smart thing and high-tailing it back to the safety of her vehicle, the woman started toward the stairs leading to the drilling floor with all the self-assurance of some royal personage whose arrival is expected. Her walk was as classy as the way she tipped her chin elegantly up in the air and ignored the men's whistles and jibes. Grant figured she was either very brave or very stupid.

He was betting on the latter.

Dropping what he was doing, he started toward the stairs with every intention of heading her off.

"Show's over," he called out to the men who had stopped laboring to ogle their visitor. "Get back to work!"

Caitlin's daddy always said they grew 'em big in Wyoming. Big and hearty. If the man blocking her way was typical, she'd have to get used to craning her neck just to look them in the eye. This particular one appeared none too friendly as he met her halfway up the stairs and positioned himself directly in her way. Clearly there was no going around this giant.

"You lost?"

It sounded more like a statement of fact than a question.

"Not at all. I know exactly where I am."

It was disturbing to hear the soft Southern drawl which attached itself to her words. Her professors had worked hard to school the "hick" out of her, but that accent still crept into her voice whenever Caitlin was feeling particularly nervous. She made a conscious effort to eradicate it as she offered the man further explanation.

"I'm the new geologist."

How wonderful it felt to say the words aloud since they not only validated her presence here but also affirmed the dream she had set her heart upon since childhood. Everyone from her mother to her high school advisor had discouraged her from pursuing such a "manly" degree. Laura Leigh had wanted her daughter to attend the same small, private institution from which she had been graduated. Caitlin had flatly refused. A college founded on the principle that young ladies needed to be culturally "finished" was definitely not for her. Only recently had her mother's alma mater allowed men on campus for anything more than uneventful mixers. Not that dating had been uppermost in Caitlin's mind. Unlike so many of the girls she had grown up around, the degree she was looking for was not her MRS.

"I said I'm the new geologist," she repeated, hoping it would lessen the tension that settled into the pit of her stomach like a bad meal.

Nothing in her college classes had prepared her for feeling so hopelessly out of place. So utterly vulnerable.

A smile played around the edges of the man's mouth as he scratched his chin thoughtfully. Caitlin could almost hear the soft rasping sound the whiskers of his five o'clock shadow made against his fingertips. A telltale tremor rippled through her body. Though she didn't expect all rig workers to be as clean-shaven as the preppy college boys she had left behind, neither was she prepared to be screened on-site by a man who looked like he would be just as at home piloting a Viking ship as driving heavy equipment. What a Hollywood producer could do with a hunk like that!

The subordinate position she held on the steps placed Caitlin at a decided disadvantage. She hoped he would attribute the flush of color in her cheeks to the summer heat—not to her discomfort at being eye level with the snap of his jeans. Her old roommate took perverse pleasure in kidding her about her sexual inexperience. Roxy said those furious blushes may as well have been a scarlet sign marking Caitlin as the oldest collegiate virgin in America.

Forcing her eyes away from the worn fly on the man's stonewashed jeans, she scanned the tight white T-shirt that emphasized both the broad plane of his chest and the breadth of his muscled forearms. Sweat stains left no doubt that these muscles had been earned the old-fashioned way, not in some posh gym with tanning beds and a personal trainer.

Taking a deep breath, she attempted to insert a note of authority into her voice. "If you'll excuse me, I'd like to get to work."

The man refused to budge. Leaning insolently against the

metal railing, he leveled a pair of electric blue eyes at her and asked, "And just who exactly hired you, Miss Scarlett?"

The smile that curled his lips made Caitlin as defensive as the derisive Southern moniker he'd tossed at her. Just because she wasn't a local didn't automatically mean she was stupid, any more than being carded at bars by doormen who claimed she looked younger than her age didn't mean she hadn't earned the college degree that gave her every right to be here. After enduring four years in traditionally male-dominated classes and having to fight for every ounce of respect owed her, Caitlin wasn't easily intimidated.

"I was hired by the owner, *Rhett*, and I'm certainly not going to show you my diploma to get by," she snapped impatiently.

Caitlin's ire only deepened the dimples on either side of the man's arrogant smile. Hoisting a huge steel-toed boot on the top of the railing, the Viking positioned his leg across the stairs like a gate. Had he actually snorted in mirth at her reference to her college diploma? She wasn't sure which bothered her more—the sense of danger that the leering men had instilled in her with their sexist hootings or the feeling that this virile bouncer was laughing at her.

There was no hint of patience in his voice when he spoke again. "Sorry, lady. Whoever led you to believe that you had a job here has played a real mean practical joke on you. We're not hiring at the moment so the best advice I can offer you, besides dropping the snotty college attitude, is to turn that fancy rig of yours around and head back the same way you came. You'll find a public phone and directions at Lysite. You can't miss it. It's the nearest town in any direction."

Town? Surely he wasn't referring to that wide spot in the road she'd passed where a handful of buildings, most notably a couple of bars, sprouted up like loosely rooted tumbleweeds. Why, with a huff and a puff a good wind could blow the place away.

Setting her jaw in determination, Caitlin forced the words through clenched teeth. "If you don't move out of the way, mister, I'll be forced to go over your head. I'd hate to have you fired," she lied. In fact nothing would give her more pleasure than to terminate this sexist clod's position.

At that, the man threw his head back and howled with laughter. "If only you could, honey, you'd probably be doing me the biggest favor of my life. But since that's not the case, I'm going to do *you* a favor. I'll personally escort you back to your Jeep and point you in the opposite direction of trouble. Someday maybe you'll appreciate the fact that somebody was concerned enough to send you on your way with your virtue intact."

It was Caitlin's turn to snort. Drawing herself up to her full five foot six, she braced her shoulders as if preparing to run the man over like a tackling dummy. Good breeding was all that kept her from uttering the oath bubbling on the tip of her tongue.

"With a head as thick as yours," she said, spitting her words out like slick watermelon seeds, "that hard hat you're wearing must be strictly for decoration."

All pretense of gallantry vanished from the man's eyes with the swiftness of a summer storm. Jerking himself into a rigid upright position, he swept the hat in question from his head and glared at her. The fact that his thick dark hair was tousled and wet with sweat made him look no less sexy, no less imposing than a bodyguard. He typified the expression "glowering good looks."

"I don't give a damn if you're a geologist or the Pope's own emissary, a drilling rig is no place for a lady—even if I do use the term loosely," he barked, crowding down onto the step beside her.

Caitlin had to turn sideways to avoid backing down. The step was so narrow that she was sure the man could feel her heart thumping wildly inside of her chest as it brushed against his. At the contact, she felt a jolt of pure sexual energy race though her, short-circuiting the electrodes that connected her brain to her body. Frozen in place, she gaped at him as if seeing Frankenstein's monster come to life.

"I'm not going to tell you again," he said. "If you don't turn around right now and clear out on your own, I'll be forced to bodily remove you from the premises."

It took every bit of Caitlin's self-restraint to keep from slapping the smirk right off that handsome face. She didn't doubt for a moment that he meant what he said. An image of herself slung over this barbarian's shoulder like so much chattel to the crew's gleeful delight made her shudder. She had worked too hard and come too far to be dismissed in such a comic, brutal manner.

This wasn't at all how she had envisioned her first day on the job.

One of the men gathered about the drilling floor hollered out, "Betcha Harry wouldn't be so quick to run off such a fine-looking geologist."

"Don't mind him, sweetheart. Come on up," entreated another. "You can check out my rocks anytime!"

Grant whipped his head around like a rattlesnake ready to strike. Just what he didn't need—an audience to observe some saucy college girl bent on undermining his authority. The fact that the crew was enjoying the show only served to strengthen his resolve to get her out of here before all hell broke loose. That and the fact that she was trying to blink back the moisture in her eyes.

Damn it all to hell! The one thing in the world Grant couldn't handle was a woman's tears. A moment ago he was contemplating whether to hoist her over his shoulder. Now suddenly he found himself wanting to enfold the poor little thing in his arms and protect her from the crudity of men who saw but one thing in a woman. Looking at the youthful hope, the unquenchable resolve burning in this girl's eyes, he realized such chivalry would be as useless as trying to stop a moth from immolating itself on a bare lightbulb.

"I thought I told you to get back to work!" Grant called out over his shoulder.

If he were ever able to pinpoint who'd uttered that crude piece of innuendo that had this pretty little thing blushing six unbecoming shades of red, he intended to personally throttle him.

Pace yourself, he reminded himself. After all, he could only be expected to deal with one emergency at a time.

"Last chance, lady," Grant growled, putting his hands on her shoulders. "You can do this with or without dignity, but one thing's for certain—you're not staying here. It's not safe or smart."

Caitlin flinched as if she had been branded by his touch. Ignited by womanly indignation, fire snapped in eyes the color of precious emeralds.

"Do you have any idea who you're talking to?" She punctuated the question by thumping a finger against the middle of his chest.

Dark clouds turned his blue eyes as gray as gunmetal. Caitlin suspected that had she been a man, he would have snapped her index finger off at the joint.

"Do *you?*" he snarled in reply.

"What's all the trouble about up there?" bellowed a familiar voice.

Grant looked down to see Paddy stumbling out of the trailer below. Looking as grumpy as a grizzly awakened from a sound sleep, the older man provided a welcome diversion from the trouble at hand.

His voice heavy with irony, Grant hollered to his partner over the side of the rig. "You're just in time. Maybe you can use some of that famous Irish charm to explain to this doll that an oil rig is no place for a woman."

Much to Grant's surprise, Paddy's mere presence was able to accomplish what all of his stern directives had not. It got the woman moving. In fact she took off down the stairs two at a time, her speed giving her the uncanny appearance of actually flying.

Her voice rose over the hum of the machinery as she cried out in unrestrained joy, "Daddy!"

Two

A moment later Grant watched dumbfounded as the woman who claimed to be their new geologist launched herself into Paddy's outstretched arms. This time he didn't bother swearing under his breath. His eloquence colored the air around him blue.

No wonder she had looked so familiar. Paddy had been sticking cherished photographs of his darling baby girl under Grant's nose for the better part of a decade. Long ago he had tired of hearing how wonderful the "little princess" was. Paddy's pride and joy, Caitlin occupied much of her daddy's thoughts. When Paddy had a couple of beers in him, she dominated most of the conversation as well.

Grant didn't have to personally know Caitlin Flynn to dislike her. To hear Paddy talk, she was the toast of Texas, a regular debutante just like her mother—that coldhearted witch who had left him because he lacked "culture" and had spine enough to resist her efforts to turn him into something he could never be. Of course, Grant didn't claim to know the whole story. Even after ten years, Paddy's wounds were still so raw he seldom spoke of the woman who had broken his heart. The woman after whom he had named his company. Most people were under the impression that L.L. Drilling stood for Lucky Lady, but once over a six-pack of beer Paddy had shared with Grant the little-known fact that it was actually Laura Leigh who had inspired the name.

The only thing women had ever inspired in Grant's life was grief.

Perhaps that was why it was so hard for him to understand Paddy's preoccupation with turning out a daughter in the exact same mold as her mother. It was his understanding that nothing Paddy did was ever good enough for the fragile, city-bred bride who found the open spaces of Wyoming as terrifying as marriage to a man with oil under his fingernails. Grant never put much stock into that old axiom about opposites attracting. Personally he wasn't sold on the tired, overrated institution of marriage, but as far as he was concerned, the more similar one's background and interests, the better the chance a relationship had of surviving.

There was no denying that he had always been fascinated by those photos of Paddy's dark-haired, green-eyed angel, but the truth of the matter was, even in photos, Caitlin struck him as being a snob. Maybe it was all those little white matching gloves and anklets in her childhood pictures or perhaps the one of her sitting sidesaddle in an English riding competition in her adolescence that gave him the impression early on that this girl was too darned smug for her own good.

It galled him to think of all the privileges she took for granted.

For what Paddy had spent on his daughter's Ivy League college degree Grant could have easily paid his way to a state university many times over. Fate hadn't been so kind to him as it had been to fresh-faced Little Miss Texas. *His* chances of ever going to college had gone up in smoke with the explosion that had killed his father. When all was said and done, Grant supposed that he was probably a better man for not having been born with a silver spoon in his mouth. Still, it was hard sometimes not to be bitter, but he reminded himself again how useless it was belaboring the past.

As far as he could tell psychiatrists were the only ones to benefit from such counterproductive thinking, and they had to be *paid* exorbitant fees to listen to people whine about things that couldn't be changed. What with his father's premature death, his mother's suicide, and his Aunt Edna's treachery, Grant was sure the modern school of psychology would have a field day with him. He figured he'd warrant an entire chapter entitled, "Real Men with Honorary Degrees from the School of Hard Knocks." He wanted no more part of such psychological pity patter than he did the kind of superficial chatter he supposed Caitlin had perfected at sorority parties.

Despite the blood tie connecting Paddy to his daughter, Grant couldn't bring himself to believe his friend would circumvent his authority by hiring Caitlin without so much as asking him first. Even as softhearted as he was, surely Paddy had sense enough to know that a drilling rig was no place for the daughter he was certain was as pure as virgin falling snow. A likely story, in Grant's opinion, only if she went to college at a convent. The probability of any woman who looked like that remaining chaste into her twenties was even slimmer than his chance of hitting that deep pocket of oil and salvaging this godforsaken company any time soon.

Grant wiped the back of his neck with a red bandanna and considered the scene playing on the ground below him. It appeared his hellish day was about to get even hotter. From Caitlin's animated gesticulations, he imagined she was at this very moment describing to her father just how "beastly" his hired hand had treated her. A smile played upon Grant's lips. He wondered how she would react to the news that he was more than just some menial hireling. If it weren't for the fact that her certain histrionics might well drive a wedge between him and the man he had come to think of as a father, Grant would have looked forward to the performance. *The Blue Blood and the Redneck.*

No doubt it had a certain Hollywood ring to it.

Stuffing his bandanna back into his hip pocket, he decided it was pointless postponing the inevitable. As hesitant as he was about breaking up this touching family reunion, it was time to officially make the formal acquaintance of Her Royal Highness, the Princess of Petulance.

Caitlin was so moved by the sight of her father that she momentarily forgot all about those odious men and their Viking leader, Redneck the Terrible. Safe in her daddy's arms, her only thought was of how glad she was to be with him again. For so many years, distance and her mother's judgment had kept them apart. Now at last a college graduate, Caitlin was free to do with her life as she wished—and what she wanted more than anything else in the world was to make up for lost time with the father she adored.

Oh, she had taken Psych 101 and knew that most girls idolized their daddies. She also knew that eventually the harsh light of reality shattered their childish beliefs that their fathers were invincible. But what she could never get her professor to understand was that *her* father really was that which John Wayne personified in all those wonderful old movies: the most honorable, kindhearted, heroic man who ever lived.

Tears filled her eyes as she pressed her ear against his heart and took comfort in its steady beat. She felt all of ten years old again in her father's arms. Safe, secure, and happy. Caitlin was determined not to let anything pull her from the refuge of those arms ever again.

''As much as I hate to interrupt this touching moment, we really do have work to do around here.''

Grant's voice sounded like the gravel crunching beneath his feet as he approached. He moved slowly, hoping to give them enough time to disengage from the tearful embrace that twisted his guts into a tight, tangled knot.

God above, what he would give to hug his own father one more time!

Taking the pained look on his face for disapproval, Caitlin

gave him a disdainful once-over. Her voice was laced with righteous indignation when she turned back to her father. "Daddy, I'd appreciate it if you would tell this, this...two-bit tool pusher just who is in charge around here."

The self-satisfied smirk she tossed Grant's direction indicated a little groveling to keep his job was in order.

"Yeah, Daddy," Grant mimicked, disregarding her haughtiness with a sarcastic grin that deepened the dimple in his chin. Crossing his muscled arms across his chest, he continued as if she weren't there at all. "Since your daughter isn't inclined to listen to me, would you mind telling her exactly who is responsible for the hiring and firing of personnel in this company?"

Paddy was grinning as he shook his head. "If you two kids would stop fighting long enough, I'd like to introduce you to one another. Maybe then we can go about getting things squared up to everybody's satisfaction."

Though that seemed highly unlikely, both Caitlin and Grant felt duly chastised by Paddy's use of the word *kids*. Instead of grown-up men and women, independent and capable in their own right, they may as well have been errant siblings squabbling in the back of the family vehicle on one of those interminable vacations that tests a parent's sanity.

Eager to be the first to appear reasonable and adult, Caitlin patted her father's arm soothingly. "You're right, of course. And if *somebody* would just calm down for a minute, I'm sure you can straighten *him* out in no time flat."

Ignoring Grant's pointed glare, Caitlin focused her attention upon her father's pallor. He looked older than she remembered. It was no secret that Paddy scorned diets devoid of meat and potatoes, and according to him, exercise was just for people who didn't have real jobs that demanded physical exertion. Winding her arm through his, Caitlin scrutinized his features more closely. The broken blood vessels in his nose and the sweat on his brow made her nervous. Excessive heat and stress was a bad combination for a man of his age and temperament.

"Are you trying to give my father a heart attack with all your theatrics?" she hissed at Grant.

"Me?" he gasped in disbelief. "You come flouncing onto this rig like the Queen of the Nile, prancing around in front of the crew in those tight jeans acting like you own the place, and I'm the one who's upset your father?"

Caitlin's mouth flew open. "Flounced!" she repeated, taking obvious exception to his choice of words. "Pranced!"

Grant cupped a hand to his ear. "Do I hear an echo?"

"Now, now, children..." Paddy's sigh bespoke a weariness that was bone deep. "It wouldn't do to have us airing out our family laundry in front of the crew, now would it? I suggest we take our differences inside the trailer away from prying eyes, and sift this all out over a nice, cold beer."

Caitlin pressed her lips together in a disapproving line. "You know what the doctor said about your triglycerides."

"You're not about to start that nonsense again, are you?" Paddy asked. He glanced toward Grant and explained in a note of exasperation. "She likes to nag me about my diet. Says my cholesterol, triglycerides, and conglomerates are all too high."

The misapplication of his words brought a smile to Caitlin's face. Despite his grumbling, she knew that her father loved the way she fussed over him.

"You know it's for your own good," she persisted.

"Piss-h, posh." Paddy quickly amended the intended oath and shot Grant a warning glance. Clearly he didn't want his lily-white princess discovering her daddy had the vernacular of a seasoned drill sergeant.

Grant rolled his eyes. As far as he could tell, this little gal's power was nothing short of amazing. In less than fifteen minutes, she had his crew acting like wild, hormone-imbalanced adolescents and Paddy like a sainted father straight off some serial from the early days of television. It was sickening to watch and reason enough to reinforce Grant's resolve to harden his heart against all women. Those like Paddy's Laura Leigh and his own mother only desert you when times get tough. Those like Aunt Edna use trickery and guile to get what they want. Suspecting that Caitlin straddled both categories, Grant wanted nothing more from her than distance.

He certainly did not want to be trapped in close quarters with her. Those cat-green eyes studying him as if he were her next meal made him way too nervous. Grant suspected that if she were to ever train those phenomenal eyes on him the way she did her father, as if he were the best thing God ever created, he would crumble into pieces like the proverbial Gingerbread Man. And like that desperate little cookie in his favorite children's story, Grant was determined to run, run as fast he could from this cunning little fox.

"Your daughter's not the only one worried about your health," he said slowly as if measuring his words into a beaker. "I don't think you need a beer either, and considering the fact that Harry just got canned for drinking on the job, I can hardly show up on the drilling floor with beer on my breath."

Much to Grant's surprise, Paddy conceded with an affable nod of his head.

"Good point. You and Caitlin can have sodas instead." Without waiting to hear any argument, he put an arm affectionately around his daughter's shoulders and directed her toward the trailer. To the delight of the crew, he called out over his shoulder, "Take a break, boys!"

Trailing miserably behind them, Grant couldn't help recalling that old adage about blood being thicker than water. It fit like a fist in his throat.

He tried not to focus on the tight fit of those designer jeans across her trim backside as she sashayed through the sagebrush in front of him. Grant knew he shouldn't resent Paddy focusing all his attention on the daughter he'd seen so infrequently over the years, but knowing and feeling were two completely different things. Jealousy reared its ugly head. With the return of the prodigal child, Grant expected Paddy to ask him to kill the fatted calf any minute now.

"Don't worry," he heard Caitlin reassure Paddy. "Before

you know it, my cooking will replace that petroleum in your veins with healthy red and white blood cells.''

''More'n likely you mean blue blood,'' Grant mumbled stepping around them to open the door. Despite his personal feelings toward this hellcat, he was bound to give courtesy its due.

''*Such* a gentleman,'' Caitlin quipped with a deprecating little moue.

Certain that one good kiss would be all it would take to wipe that smirk off those pouty lips, Grant imagined bending her swanlike neck back, pressing his lips against hers, and taming that fiery temper with a single mind-numbing kiss. A mere taste of his potency was sure to leave this pretty little princess limp and willing in his arms. After hanging around with college boys, Grant very much doubted whether Caitlin could handle a real man.

As if trying to shut out such disturbing thoughts, Grant slammed the door behind him. He blamed lack of sleep for the wayward turn his thoughts had taken. Lack of sleep and a decided lack of female companionship. The next time he got to town, Grant vowed to remedy that situation. Even if he *liked* Caitlin Flynn, which he decidedly did not, he valued his relationship with Paddy far too much to screw things up by even *thinking* of becoming involved with his precious daughter. Not that Caitlin would risk a nosebleed to look down from her pedestal upon mere oil field trash such as himself.

Stepping in from the intense sunlight outside, Caitlin needed a moment to adjust to the relative dimness of the trailer. Dust motes danced before her eyes. She was surprised to see that the trailer was relatively tidy, though hardly luxurious. Dishes were washed and drying in the wire rack over the sink, clothes were picked up, magazines were stacked neatly beside a sturdy couch of blotchy tweed blends, and an afghan she had lovingly made for her father for Christmas several years ago was draped neatly over the back of a black vinyl recliner. Considering the gritty conditions of the location, Caitlin was impressed. Her father had never struck her as being a particularly fastidious housekeeper.

"Have a seat, darlin'," Paddy said, pointing to a small kitchenette table and two chairs.

Caitlin obliged, and Grant took an extra folding chair from the closet and set it up directly across the table from her. They exchanged cold glances while Paddy drew an old metal tray of ice cubes from the refrigerator and unceremoniously cracked it on the counter. A minute later he set two glasses of pop and a bottle of ice-cold beer on a table so flimsy that it wobbled beneath the elbows he propped there an instant later.

"There now," he exclaimed, joining them. "Isn't this cozy?"

Too cozy, Caitlin thought, drawing herself up primly in her chair so that her knees wouldn't brush against Grant's. Those long legs of his could no more be contained beneath the tiny circumference of that table than his ego could be contained within the band of the hard hat he placed between them like some symbolic barrier.

Paddy raised his beer in a salute and took a deep, satisfying draught.

"What'dya say we start over? Caitlin, I'd like you to meet Grant Davis."

Davis. Davis. Davis... The name sounded oddly familiar. Caitlin searched her memory but couldn't place it. She seriously doubted whether he was related to any of the San Antonio Davises that her mother set such store by.

"And, Grant, this is my daughter, Caitlin."

When this introduction was met with nothing but loud, hostile silence, Paddy's good humor exploded. "Just what exactly is the problem here? I can't imagine why a friendly visit from my favorite daughter would inspire such animosity in you, Grant, or how—"

Grant turned to Caitlin in disbelief. "Then this is just a social visit? You led me to believe that... Well, in that case, I'm sorry that I acted like such a—"

Interrupting his apology with an angry wave of her hand,

Caitlin focused her response upon her father. "No, it isn't *just* a visit. I'm here to go to work for you, Dad. I hope you didn't spend a fortune to send me off to college just to pat me on the head and send me off like some cute little puppy. You didn't, did you?"

"Of course not," Paddy sputtered. "It's just that I don't think we're looking for a geologist, honey."

"We're not," Grant confirmed tersely.

"Yes, you are," Caitlin countered. Eyeing her father's beer disapprovingly, she crossed her fingers behind her back and blurted out a plausible, abbreviated version of the truth. "I ran into your old one down the road a ways. He said to tell you that his services had suddenly become indispensable to another company that was paying better. I took the liberty of telling him that you already had a replacement—me!"

"What?" bellowed Grant, jumping to his feet.

He had been wondering where Doug was. The fellow prided himself on his punctuality, if not actual ability. Finding it hard to believe that a rival company had poached him, Grant's eyes narrowed. There really was no polite way of suggesting that Paddy's daughter was a liar.

Shaking his head solemnly, Paddy scolded, "You really shouldn't have done that, honey."

"Yes, I should've." Caitlin placed her elbows on the table, cupped her chin in her hands, and leaned forward intently. She looked her father square in the eye. "Look, there's no reason for you to pay somebody to do what I'm willing to do for free. It's the least I can do for all you've done for me. Besides, I want to. Badly. Not to mention that I have a vested interest in *our* business myself. And it is the perfect opportunity for us to spend some time together."

"Caitlin, darlin'," Paddy replied with a note of pleading in his voice. "A rig's no place for a beautiful girl such as yourself. I wanted you to go to college so you'd never have to do hard physical labor like me. Like your grandmother, God rest her soul, a poor charwoman working her fingers to the bone, saving all her hard-earned pennies to send her sons to America for a better life. That's what I sent you to college for, a better life.''

Taking her manicured hands into his own, he cradled them gently. ''Hands such as these are meant for a laboratory, for diamond rings, for holding my grandbabies some day. Not for grubbing in the dirt with a bunch of lewd men out in the middle of nowhere.''

The tenderness her father's words inspired disappeared at the implication that she couldn't take care of herself. It seemed to Caitlin that she had spent her entire life trying to convince others just how capable she was. Foolishly she had hoped a degree would eliminate the need for this very conversation. However, she understood that lashing out at her father in feminist rage would get her nowhere fast. Instead she took an altogether different route to getting her way.

''I appreciate your concern, but what I really need is a job, not kid-glove protection. The market isn't exactly booming for inexperienced college graduates. What with downsizing, companies are hiring experienced geologists for about the same pay as entry-level workers. If I ever hope to get a better job than flipping burgers at some fast-food chain, I'll have to get some experience first. The way I figure it, the best way for me to get experience is to work with the best. And that's why I came to you.''

Grant saw something soften in Paddy's eyes. He had to hand it to her. Caitlin had a real knack for winding her old man as tightly around her little finger as the chain around the rig's rotary table.

Paddy ran his hand through his still thick shock of graying hair. ''Well, since you put it that way…''

''Don't forget about the financial benefit to the company. They don't come any cheaper than me.'' The smile Caitlin flashed her father was warm enough to completely melt the last of the ice in Grant's soda. He knew he had to intervene fast.

''And don't *you* forget,'' he interrupted in a burst of disgust, ''that I'm the one who does the hiring around here. And at the present time I'm not inclined to hire a slip of a girl for any position.''

"Now, now," Paddy said, taking another draught of his beer. "Let's not be so hasty, son."

Son!

The word ricocheted through Caitlin's brain like a sniper's bullet. How dare her father use that word with this arrogant jerk! Deep down she suspected that Paddy secretly had always wanted a son. A son to work with side by side. A son to turn the business over to when it became too much for him. A son he could be proud of. All her life Caitlin had tried to make up for her sex by being the best she could at everything she undertook. She couldn't help wondering whether Paddy would have been so willing to grant full custody to her mother had she been a son instead of a daughter.

"How dare you try to tell my father how to run *his* business?" she snapped at Grant. "If I were him, I'd run you off on the spot for such impudence."

Still standing, Grant leaned his considerable height over her and answered in a laconic tone, "I dare because I'm not just some lackey you can push around at will. Like it or not, I'm your daddy's right-hand man, and I have as much at stake here as he does."

Three

Determined to look Grant eye to eye when she confronted him, Caitlin leapt to her feet. Her chair clattered to the floor behind her.

"Is *right-hand man* your official title, or is that just a fancy way of saying you've wormed your way into a heart too kind for its own good?" She attempted to lessen the difference in their heights by standing on tiptoe and anchoring her hands to her hips for ballast. "Do you expect me to believe that my father simply turned the running of his business over to you because you graciously volunteered to be the son he never had? Let me assure you, mister. I'm not about to stand by and watch you destroy what it's taken my father an entire lifetime to build."

"Caitlin, stop it!" Paddy's voice cut through the air like the crack of a bullwhip. "Stop it right now before you make a bigger fool out of yourself than you already have."

Tears stung her eyes. Caitlin could count on one hand the times that her father had raised his voice to her. To be thus admonished in front of this outsider was almost more than she could bear.

Accusation laced her voice as she demanded an answer. "How can you just sit there and let your employee treat me with such contempt? The next thing I know he'll be telling me that you want to make him a full-fledged partner."

Paddy flinched from the betrayal glistening in his daughter's eyes.

Grant railed against it.

Was it so unimaginable that he could have procured his boss's high regard by any but underhanded means? Paddy had promised the entire crew a bonus if they could make this hole pay out before the deadline. He had, in fact, intimated that there would be an extra special something awaiting the man who worked the hardest to prove himself as he went through the ranks. Though no one knew exactly what the prize was, Grant hoped it involved enough money to secure that ranch that he'd been dreaming of for so very long.

Caitlin's overly emotional reaction to the idea that her father might share the burdens of the business by offering his second in command a chance at a partnership only served to underscore Grant's opinion of women. Any man unfortunate enough to ever forget that the "fairer" sex was only out for personal gain was destined to be very sorry indeed. All that hype about Caitlin's coming here just to be close to her daddy was nothing more than a convenient cover to check up on *her* assets.

The inheritance factor was just one more thing for Grant to hold against her. But then, what could he expect a little princess from the suburbs to understand of earning one's keep by the sweat of your brow? Of the pride that comes of making something of yourself out of the ashes of defeat? Of loving a man like Paddy Flynn not for the width of the financial security net he could weave beneath you, but instead for his honesty and decency?

"I thought they were supposed to teach you in college to find out the facts before jumping to conclusions," Grant commented dryly.

A muscle along his jawline throbbed out his frustration as he took full measure of the pretty little thing who'd just called him a con man. Any man with the audacity to make such an accusation would have found himself cheek to cheek with the nearest wall.

Arms up in the air, Paddy jumped into the middle of the fracas. His complexion was even ruddier than usual as he attempted arbitration. "Caitlin, surely you remember my speaking of Keith Davis, my partner from years ago. Grant's his son."

A frown creased Caitlin's brow. Recognition glimmered beneath the surface of her memory like a dark fish rising from the depths.

"Keith Davis... Wasn't he the man who..."

"The man," Grant supplied, "who was killed in the explosion that nearly bankrupted this company years ago. The explosion that left second-degree burns over fifty percent of your father's body."

Caitlin turned her attention upon her father. "The one that caused you and Mother to—"

Words failed her as she searched Paddy's stricken eyes for an answer to the question that had obsessed her for years. Growing up, the subject of her parents' separation had been expressly taboo. When she was younger, Caitlin had found a photograph in her mother's album of a strange mummy-like creature staring back at her from a hospital bed. Laura Leigh had curtly explained that it was Paddy, shortly before she made up her mind to leave him.

When with typical adolescent candor Caitlin expressed the opinion that it was unbelievably cold of her mother to abandon her father in such a state, Laura Leigh had replied cryptically, "We were both burned in that fire, Caitlin. Someday when you're older, maybe I'll try explaining it to you."

For some reason that day never came. Caitlin hoped that with the passage of time, the truth would finally come out. Unfortunately, Paddy had no more intention of pillaging the past than her mother.

"Let's leave old times well enough alone except to say that Grant's father was the best friend I ever had. In fact I never met a better man—until the day his son showed up at one of my rigs. Despite the fact he held me personally responsible for his father's death, he said he was willing to learn the business from the bottom up. The only thing he asked of me was a paycheck. Promised to earn his keep, and, by God, girl, he has more than done that."

It was impossible to miss the effect these words had upon Grant. He stood perceptibly taller, and the moisture clouding his eyes was clearly an embarrassment to him.

Coming from a man not easily given to compliments, Caitlin was aware how rare such praise was. What *she* would have given to hear her father speak so highly of her! Unbidden, a seed of jealousy sprouted in her heart for the man who had somehow managed to usurp her hitherto unshakable position as the apple of her father's eye.

"Am I to take it then that you somehow feel duty bound to Keith's son?" Caitlin asked. Unloosed from a throat tight with emotion, her voice sounded high and strained.

"Contractually I'm not obligated to anyone. But when you consider that Grant came here on his own to bust his butt for a company on the brink of bankruptcy, yes, I think it's fair to say that I feel an obligation to him," Paddy responded shortly.

Caitlin flinched against the reproof in her father's voice. Then hardened herself against it. However nicely Paddy gilded it, something didn't sound quite right in his abbreviated explanation. Until proven otherwise, Grant would remain suspect in her mind. The thought intensified her desire to stick around and see what exactly this man was up to.

"Let me get this straight," she said, gesturing toward her father with graceful, long fingers. "You blame yourself for an act of God, then spend time teaching this bleeding heart everything he wants to know about the oil business out of sheer pity, and you can't so much as give your own daughter a solitary chance to earn her keep around here?"

Paddy was not a man accustomed to having his judgment

questioned. "It wasn't pity," he snapped. "Grant's proven himself many times over."

Despite the anger Caitlin's question aroused in him, Grant nonetheless considered it fair. In fact looking back on it, he couldn't think of anyone presenting a more pitiful image than he had that day he'd arrived with his hat in hand, humbly asking to be taught the tools of the very trade that had claimed his father's life. Having targeted Paddy in his mind for years as the cause of that fatal accident, it had been all he could do to keep from throttling his father's partner. The last thing he'd expected was to ever like the old codger who managed somehow to take him in without compromising his dignity by offering him not a hand out, but a hand up.

Grateful that Paddy had glossed over years of heartache with one broad, sweeping stroke, Grant nevertheless could not forget that there was far more to the story of how their partnership came about than Paddy was telling. It was just like Paddy to leave the telling of that to him when and if he ever decided to share it.

"If you're trying to put a price tag on what was owed me," Grant growled, "you'll have to tell me the going rate to replace a father."

Caitlin drew her breath in sharply as her heart cried out the answer to Grant's inquiry. No amount of money in the world! As difficult as it had been growing up in a broken home, Caitlin loved both her parents dearly and couldn't imagine life without either one.

For the first time since meeting this man, she felt an inkling of sympathy for him. He may look as impervious as a Roman gladiator now, but she mentally calculated his age and figured that he must have still been in high school when tragedy befell his family. Her throat closed around the image of a beautiful, dark-haired teenager acting as his father's pallbearer. And of a tearful, bereft mother leaning on him for support. It was Caitlin's understanding that the mere thought of losing Paddy in such a hellish manner had been enough to compel her mother to abandon the one true love of her life. Maintaining that she was too young to be a widow, like poor Cissy Davis, Laura Leigh had shortly thereafter packed her bags and headed back to the security of her parents' home in San Antonio.

Caitlin bit the inside of her mouth in a nervous habit that survived her childhood. "I didn't mean it to sound like that. It's just that I feel obligated to look after my father's interests. It is awfully strange that he hasn't mentioned you to me before."

"As much as I appreciate your concern," Paddy interjected with a crooked smile. "I'm a grown man accustomed to making my own decisions. Maybe I didn't feel the need to explain myself to you. Then—or now."

With that, he ran his hands through his silver hair. "This conversation is over. The only thing left to decide is what to do with you, young lady."

Fighting the tears that welled up in her eyes, Caitlin set her jaw in the same determined way that her father had of leading with his chin whenever things looked their bleakest. She was not about to come all this way just to be brushed off. There was far more at stake here than just a job.

Her self-worth was quivering on the line.

"I'll tell you what you can do with me," she countered, each word an articulated bullet. "You can back off and let me do my job!"

Grant had to admire the lady's grit. Having expected her to employ the age-old female tools of alternately crying and pouting, he was struck by Caitlin's fortitude in standing up to Paddy Flynn, the terror of drillers and corporate giants alike. It aroused in him a grudging respect.

Suppressing a smile, he imagined her reaction to the strictly male observation that she was indeed very beautiful when she was mad. He was mesmerized by the attention she paid the gold locket nestled in the hollow of her throat. The way she was stroking it so lovingly made Grant wonder if it was some kind of a magic talisman. Maybe a religious medal. Perhaps a lucky charm to protect her from catastrophes, assorted imaginary ills, and hard-hatted villains.

Neither Caitlin's voice nor her resolve quavered as she continued the fight to get her way. "I'll make you a deal. I'll offer my services totally free of charge for one month. If I can't prove my worth to you in that time, I'll accept your decision to replace me. No questions asked. No hard feelings."

"No way!" Grant exploded. Alarm bells were sounding in his head. One only had to watch the way Paddy was thoughtfully scratching his chin to see all hope of banishing this woman from the premises go up in a magician's poof of smoke. "I don't have time to be baby-sitting some college kid whose knowledge of an oil field is limited to what some dried-up old professor asked on a midterm."

No matter how pretty she is! he added silently to himself.

"No one asked you to," she countered, twisting her necklace around her index finger and wishing it was the man's thick neck instead. "Besides, I don't see that you have much choice in the matter. Whether you like it or not, you need a geologist. It's going to take some time to line another one up. Why not at least let me fill in during the interim? What have you got to lose?" she asked, her eyes flashing him a challenge in emeralds.

Besides my sanity and the friendship with your father that I value above everything else in the world?

"Just my time, this oil rig, the entire business, and my physical well-being when the crew decides you might make an interesting diversion some lonely night," Grant snorted with an angry wave of his hand.

A shiver raced through Caitlin at the thought. "I can take care of myself," she retorted, not bothering to explain about the defense class she had taken in college for physical education credit. If the need were ever to arise, she knew how to fell a man like a tree.

Grant rolled his eyes at this assurance. "I'm sure you can— at a sorority party or a poetry reading. But we're not talking about the latest trends in social awareness here. This is an oil rig, not a library or an office. You can't protect yourself here with a thick book and that withering look you've perfected."

A degree in geology hadn't prepared her for dealing with such hardheadedness. "Maybe I should have majored in archeology," Caitlin murmured sweetly.

Grant's eyebrows arched into question marks.

"That way I would have been better prepared to deal with such an archaic male attitude. I don't know why you have a chip on your shoulder the size of the state of Wyoming, but it seems like you're just afraid that I might be good at what I do."

"What I'm afraid of," Grant clarified with an angry jab at the air, "is that your father won't be able to let his own daughter go when the time comes."

Paddy started to point out that he was in the room and capable of speaking for himself, but Caitlin cut him off before the first syllable was out of his mouth.

"You've made it perfectly clear that you are the one in charge of hiring and firing. If in a month's time you haven't changed your mind about me, I'll abide by your decision. Daddy won't have anything to say about it."

"Sounds more than fair to me." There was a hint of admiration in Paddy's voice.

Grant's groan was of theatric proportions. "I don't like it."

"What you mean is that you don't like me," Caitlin observed. "You don't have to. You just have to work with me."

She stuck out her hand and forced a decision, one way or the other. "Do we have a deal?"

Thinking he'd rather kiss a rattlesnake than shake her hand, Grant's voice dripped with sarcasm. "Like I have a choice."

He looked to Paddy for support but instead found a happy smile of anticipation plastered on his old friend's face. This little vixen had indeed positioned him upon the horns of a dilemma. Either way he jumped, he could expect to be gored. Grant considered the small, manicured hand dangling in the air in front of him. He shook his head in disgust. As Paddy had pointed out earlier, such hands were not intended for the kind of hard work to which this woman was so blithely pledging herself. Grant hoped she understood that on this rig she would be asked to pitch in and do more than what might fall into the scope of a written job description. Real life wasn't as orderly as college professors were apt to lead one to believe.

Damned if he didn't feel the strongest urge to bend his lips to those clean, polished fingertips and kiss them. He shook his head at the medieval image that evoked. Both Paddy and Caitlin were looking at him, waiting for his response.

Reluctantly he took Caitlin's hand in his.

He was not prepared for the impact her touch had on him. A thousand volts of electricity surged between them. Grant knew that Caitlin felt it too by the way her eyes grew wide, exposing her shock for the length of two full seconds.

Sheer willpower alone gave him the strength to pull his hand away from hers.

A telltale blush stained Caitlin's cheeks as she looked straight into his eyes and told the most prodigious lie he'd ever heard. "You won't be sorry."

Four

"I don't want to inconvenience anyone," Caitlin insisted. "Really."

Grant tried not to gag as he watched her work her father over. The little lady had perfected the art of female persuasion with an adoring look that had Paddy doing back flips to accommodate her. It didn't take an enormous stretch of the imagination to envision a horde of pimple-faced, preppy schoolboys falling all over themselves for a chance to carry the Princeton Princess's books across campus. The poor suckers.

Grant's observation that their small trailer was going to be mighty cramped, considering the fact that there were only two bedrooms available didn't seem to faze Caitlin in the least.

"I'll just have to sleep on the couch then," she responded with the kind of magnanimous sincerity Grant considered worthy of Hollywood's recognition.

"Fine with me," he grumbled. He saw no reason to give up *his* bed for this spoiled college brat. The least a man should expect after putting in long, demanding hours of physical labor was a firm mattress. The very least.

His words were drowned out by Paddy's firm protest.

"Absolutely not," he declared. "If anyone's going to sleep on the couch, darlin', it's going to be me."

Grant groaned. Paddy had no more intention of sleeping on that couch than he did of using a rock for a pillow. Greatly amused by the older man's grandstanding, he watched him forage helplessly in the closet for bedding, one hand pressed dramatically to the small of his back. Grant was tempted to applaud the performance.

"Don't even think of it, Dad!" Caitlin exclaimed, successfully wrestling him away from the closet and into the easy chair.

"I won't have you sleeping on the couch and that's all there is to that," her father puffed chivalrously. "It wouldn't be right for a beautiful young lady to be without her privacy."

Had Paddy's pallor not been of such real concern to him, Grant might have enjoyed the show a good while longer. As it was, he was too fond of the older man to ever actually allow him to jeopardize his health by sleeping on a sagging sofa. It would not, however, have bothered him in the least to save the privilege for Caitlin. As far as he was concerned, a bed of nails would be good enough for her Royal Eminence.

In the midst of their argument, Grant slipped away unnoticed. When he returned a few minutes later carrying enough heavy suitcases to tax his considerable muscles, father and daughter were still engaged in a rousing game of martyrdom.

"Enough already," Grant groused on his way through to deposit Caitlin's luggage in *his* room. "Think you packed enough for what promises to be a *short* stay?"

Caitlin refused to dignify his sarcasm with a response. Instead she merely stepped out of his way, "I had every intention of doing that myself, and I hope you know it wasn't my idea to put you out of your room."

"Save it for the Academy Awards," he grumbled, not even bothering to slow down.

* * *

Caitlin hated letting such an odious man do her any favors. Having fought hard for the right to be treated as an equal, she preferred carrying her own baggage around—so to speak. She did not want to begin this particular job in debt to Grant Davis for anything as chivalrous as opening a door or carrying in her belongings. She was keenly aware that he wasn't doing this out of fondness for her but rather out of respect for her father. Antipathy emanated from every pore in his body. Since he'd made it abundantly clear that he took affront to her college degree, Caitlin made a mental note to downplay her education in his presence. Seeing how they were going to be roommates after all, she saw no sense in borrowing trouble.

"He's a good man," her father assured her.

Caitlin remained unconvinced as the sound of suitcases being dumped onto the floor resonated through thin walls.

She smiled weakly. "A regular knight in shining armor."

A minute later he was back, crossing the room in a few long strides. "I've got to get back to work," he said, pointedly checking his watch.

Opening the trailer door, Grant let in the light and the heat from outside. Caitlin was struck by the way the sunshine glowed about his body, giving the momentary illusion that she was in the presence of an angel. Not some cute little Cupid, but rather an angel warrior. Rugged St. Michael entering a fray without benefit of sword or shield.

The image disappeared with the slam of a door.

"It would mean a lot to me if you two could find a way to get along," Paddy said to his daughter. It was miserably hot inside the trailer. A bead of sweat trickled down the side of his face.

Caitlin reached over and wiped it away with a lacy handkerchief her mother had sent with her. A misty look came into Paddy's eyes as he recognized Laura Leigh's signature scent. The fragrance lingered between the two of them, an invisible reminder of the happy home they had once shared. As loudly as Paddy and Caitlin had both disavowed Laura Leigh's penchant for feminine frills and fancies, the memory that scent evoked was a rich contrast to the austerity of a small, tidy trailer sitting in the middle of the sagebrush. The sudden hint of honeysuckle bridged the gap of time, overpowering the mingled smell of dust and sweat and a river of oil rumbling silent and deep in the Earth's belly waiting to be awakened like a slumbering lover.

"I'll go unpack my things," Caitlin said. With clumsy tenderness, she placed a kiss upon the very spot where that errant drop of sweat had lingered. "Thanks for letting me stay, Daddy."

Grant's bedroom matched the rest of the trailer's decor. Neat and bleak. Walls, as bare as the top of the small cheap dresser that held his clothes, revealed no personal secrets. No single clue of Grant's past or future was evident in the room. Not that Caitlin gave a darn, she reminded herself as she opened the closet door.

A half-dozen work shirts hung there, leaving plenty of room for her own clothes, which she put up in short order. Soon all that was left was to find a suitable place for what her mother referred to as her "delicates." Caitlin hoped at least one of the dresser drawers was empty.

A funny feeling settled into the pit of her stomach as she opened the drawer which held Grant's socks and underwear. It came as a surprise to her that such a boring stack of serviceable white briefs could make her feel like such a voyeur. She slammed the drawer shut on her shame. It was a feeling too akin to lust for Caitlin to comfortably admit.

By the time she had her things in order, it was almost time for supper. Having had nothing to eat but a fruit bar and a soda since lunch, she was ravenous. Since her father had asked her to try to make an effort at getting along with Grant, Caitlin figured she could start making amends by fixing them all a nice supper.

A quick look in the refrigerator reawakened her fears that in jockeying for control of the company, Grant was actually out to kill her father. Beer seemed to be the beverage of choice. An uncovered steak coagulated in a platter of fat, a block of cheese sported the latest in fashionable molds, and an economy-size carton of eggs nestled beside a huge slab of bacon. Ketchup was the sole condiment.

The freezer compartment was jam-packed with a variety of ice cream flavors and frozen dinners, none of which carried a healthy "lite" label upon it. Instead words like *hearty* and *filling* jumped out at Caitlin. She imagined that just reading the nutritional information panel could cause one to gain five pounds.

In the pantry she found several dusty cans of fruits and vegetables hiding behind a bag of corn chips. A sack of potatoes had sprouted roots, but Caitlin figured she could salvage some of them by knocking the eyes off those that hadn't begun to rot. A couple of onions and a smattering of seasonings completed the meager reserves. It wasn't much, but it would have to do until she could get to a grocery store.

Grant hadn't taken two steps into the trailer when he was assailed by the aroma of homemade soup. Dead tired, he wanted nothing more than to take a shower, shovel one of Paddy's tasteless frozen "big man" dinners into himself, and hit the sack—or the couch as the case may be. His previously foul mood hadn't improved any since Caitlin had conned her way into his bed. The last thing he expected when he finished his shift was to be taken back in time by the smell of simmering vegetables and pungent spices.

Suddenly Grant found himself in his mother's kitchen again, marveling at what she could do with some lean wild meat, a couple of carrots, potatoes, and an onion. Best of all was the way she could magically make a lump of dough rise in the pan and make it look like an elfin cottage. The redolent smell of baking bread wafting through the house always reduced him to begging for a "taster," a crusty end piece slathered with wild honey or homemade jam or a thick slab of cheddar cheese and fresh milk. Cissy Davis's frugal dinners were a wonderment of fragrance and taste. When his father would ask what it was that made her meals so delicious, his mother would smile and say that her secret ingredient was love. And when they kissed in front of Grant, as they always did after this exchange, it seemed to him that his life was destined to go on like this forever—happy and secure.

"I hope you're hungry," Caitlin said, greeting him from the kitchen and bringing him into the present with a start.

"Hungry and tired," he admitted.

Grant couldn't remember the last time he had sat down to a home-cooked meal. Funny how a proper table setting, no matter how simple the fare, made eating seem special.

Before taking his place at the table, he attacked his hands in the bathroom sink with a bar of abrasive soap that did little to loosen the oil and grime that, like his past, seemed an indelible part of him. Wiping his hands and face with a towel, Grant paused to look at himself in the mirror. The stubble on his chin gave him a hard look, and he wondered how someone as young and delicate-looking as Caitlin dared tangle with such a tough-looking character. He secretly admired her spunk but also worried that such bravado might well land her in serious trouble with other members of the crew. Someone less of a gentleman might mistake such moxie as a challenge— with the gravest of consequences.

"It's not much," Caitlin apologized as Grant took his place at the table.

Grant started to reply that everything looked just fine when Paddy demanded to know, "Where's my steak?"

His tone was belligerent as he searched the depths of the refrigerator.

"In your soup," Caitlin explained without pausing to digest his obvious indignation. "I'm afraid tonight we'll just have to make do with soup and cheese. The bread I found was a lovely shade of bluish green. Fine for growing penicillin but not particularly appetizing. Once I get into town and pick up some groceries, you are going to begin eating healthy—whether you like it or not."

Surprised that they actually agreed on something for once, Grant grinned into the depths of his bowl. For once he wished Caitlin luck. Every time he dared to bring up the subject, Paddy searched his vocabulary for the most vivid expletives to best explain his opinion of nutritional eating.

Grant took a taste of his soup and found it delicious. He was surprised to discover Caitlin could cook. He wouldn't expect a debutante to know anything as practical as one end of a pot from the other.

"It's good," he said and grinned again at how warily she reacted to the compliment.

"I'm glad someone around here appreciates it," she replied, pointedly staring at the way Paddy was swishing his spoon around in the soup, apparently searching for tasty bits of cholesterol.

"Maybe you'll be good for something around here after all," Grant added just to see if he could get another rise out of her.

He did. Caitlin bristled up like a cat whose tail had just been stepped on.

With perfect timing, Paddy interrupted. "How's your mother?" he asked in an offhanded way that fooled no one.

"She's fine."

Grant felt a stab of pity for his mentor who was still so obviously interested in the woman who had packed up his heart when she rejoined the high-society crowd after her amusing little encounter with blue-collar life. Still Grant was too tired to pay much attention to the conversation and was eminently relieved when Caitlin refused his offer to help clean up. Excusing himself from the table, he stumbled toward the shower. If he was lucky, he told himself he wouldn't fall asleep and drown on his feet.

The water pressure was too weak to give him the kind of pulsating release that his muscles needed, but the shower was nonetheless warm and soothing. Grant felt no guilt in draining the hot water tank. It wasn't until he climbed out of the shower and was toweling himself off that he faced the quandary of his sleeping arrangements. He didn't so much as own a pair of pajamas, and the thought of sleeping in the middle of the living room in his underwear didn't much appeal to him. Not when Paddy and Caitlin were bound to want to stay up late and catch up on old times.

He glowered at himself through the steam on the bathroom mirror. "To heck with them both," he grumbled, wrapping a towel around his middle and heading toward *his* room to change into a clean pair of briefs. Whether it inconvenienced or embarrassed anyone else or not, he was going to catch some shut-eye.

Discretion won out over comfort at the last minute as Grant reached for a clean T-shirt in its usual spot in the bottom drawer. He was taken aback by the flimsy piece of lace which he fished out of his dresser instead. Apparently even his drawers were not exempt from confiscation. He couldn't so much as put a name to the sexy little froufrou dangling from his hand let alone understand what possible occasion Caitlin thought she would have to wear such a flimsy garment out in the middle of nowhere. The slick material of the camisole caught on the roughness of his fingers, and he felt a familiar, frightening tightening in his groin.

Grant groaned at the thought of satin and lace in his bedroom—and on his oil rig. As if life wasn't hard enough without courting disaster. First thing in the morning, he planned on issuing Caitlin a standard pair of overalls with the intention of covering her from chin to toe. He didn't want his crew catching so much as a peek of lace about their new geologist. Just maybe a hard hat would manage to hide that luxurious, distracting tumble of mahogany hair, he thought hopefully.

Irritated at the thought of sleeping on a raggedy old couch while Paddy's little princess slept undisturbed in his bed, Grant was tempted to put a pea under the mattress before leaving the room.

Caitlin's jaw went slack at the sight of Grant sauntering into the living room with his dark hair damp and glistening from the shower. Wearing nothing but a pair of worn jeans with a missing top snap, he was all sinew and muscles and mouth-watering masculinity. She had caught an eyeful earlier of his impressive forearms and biceps, but a T-shirt had covered the rest of his upper body. His pectoral muscles and rippled stomach seemed to Caitlin the single most beautiful thing she had ever encountered in her life. She disliked hairy chests and backs that made some men look more like bears than humans. Grant's chest had just enough to make her want to run her hands over the rock-hard contours of a body honed by hard labor.

The mere thought of sleeping in his bed made her feel wobbly. The college boys she'd dated were nothing compared to the virile hunk standing so nonchalantly before her with a lazy thumb hitched into his waistband. His imposing presence and overt sexuality hit her like a ton of testosterone. Belatedly Caitlin snapped her mouth shut.

"Sorry, folks," Grant said with an unapologetic yawn. "But if you don't mind moving off the couch, I'd like to go to bed now."

Although no innuendo was intended, just the word *bed* coming from his mouth was enough to make Caitlin redden with the weight of her inexperience. Unwilling to subject herself to the kind of teasing she had endured as a child regarding those embarrassing telltale blushes, she hopped right up.

"Of course. I'd like to get a good night's sleep for the first day on the job myself."

She started to make a quick getaway but turned around before she had gotten halfway out of the room and hurried back to drop a kiss upon her father's weathered cheek. Out of the corner of her eye she could see that Grant had missed a tiny spot on his back with that towel he had draped over his shoulder. It was all she could do to refrain from asking if he would like her to dry him off.

"Good night," she chirped and as an afterthought added from her childhood memory, "Sleep tight."

"It's the only way I'm going to keep from falling off the

sofa,'' Grant grumbled as he flattened himself against the scratchy fabric of the cushions. Too tired to belabor the fact that he'd been so neatly displaced, he attempted to go to sleep with one arm securely anchored over the back of the couch.

Caitlin could no more banish her guilt at having put him out of his bed than she could dismiss the haunting image of that incredibly sexy little trickle of water on the broad expanse of his back. She took her locket off and set it carefully on top of the dresser before slipping into her pajamas, turning off the lights, and climbing into bed. Tired as she was, sleep proved nonetheless elusive. Deep cleansing breaths were of little help. The scent that was exclusively Grant Davis tickled her nose. Caitlin rubbed the edging of the cotton sheet to her face and breathed in his very essence. A miraculous blend of woods and sagebrush and pure masculinity, it made her feel far too intimate with a man whom she was certain had every intention of firing her just as soon as he could possibly get away with it.

Five

Sunrise was painting the horizon with blazing swirls of orange, pink, and crimson when Caitlin arrived on the drilling floor. She was wearing the coveralls Grant had set out for her. He couldn't decide whether to shake his head in disgust or to chuckle in amusement at the sight. With sleeves and cuffs rolled up and a hard hat falling down to her eyes, she reminded him a little of Charlie Brown in full winter regalia, so encumbered by his clothes that he could hardly move.

Caitlin scowled when she saw him in his clean T-shirt and jeans.

A night of sleep hadn't improved either one's disposition. Exhausted, Grant had slept hard but awakened early, stiff, sore, and grumpy from sleeping on the couch. For her part, Caitlin had found it far easier blocking out the bright night lights that lit the rig up at night than the erotic, unsatisfying dreams that had curled about her like the haunting fragrance of a lost lover.

"Good morning." Fighting first-day-on-the-job jitters, she

made a conscious effort to sound as if she'd been doing this for years. "I want a core sample to see where you're at and what's going on down there."

Grant leaned idly against the brake and studied her as if someone had just pulled the string on a cute little "career exploration" doll.

"Core samples take time," he replied shortly, "and that's something I can't afford to waste. Since we only have a limited amount of time to make this hole pay off, your core sample just isn't going to happen. Sorry."

Caitlin knew he wasn't. Grinding her teeth, she forced herself to smile sweetly. "According to procedure, there is a proper way for things to be done and—"

Grant interrupted with a dismissive wave of his hand. "With all due deference to your 'procedures,' there's a whole lot more to learn about this business than what you read in books. Things like gut instinct and a nose for oil that comes only from experience."

He rubbed his chin thoughtfully, giving Caitlin the impression of an older brother searching for a slick way to ditch some tagalong younger sibling. "Tell you what. Let's make a deal," he suggested. "If you'll try to stay out of the way, I'll see what I can do to make sure you get a good recommendation and a gold star on your resume for when you decide to get a desk job some place back in Texas."

Caitlin jammed her fists into her armpits to keep from smacking him. "How dare you—"

"I dare because your daddy's not around right at the moment, but my guess is that he feels the same way that I do." Giving the appearance of a man who had wrestled demons through the night, Grant sighed deeply and rubbed the crick in his neck. "Nonetheless, I'd like to make the best of a bad situation. Since we're stuck here with each other, I don't see any reason that this arrangement can't be mutually beneficial to everyone concerned."

Caitlin's eyes narrowed as he pulled a pack of gum from

his pocket and offered her a stick. Shaking her head, she forced herself to hear him out.

He folded a piece into his mouth and pondered it a moment before continuing. "Just do as you're told, and whenever I can spare the time, I'll be glad to help you get some of that precious on-the-job training that you were crying about earlier."

Clinging desperately to her pride, Caitlin tried to keep her voice even as she attempted to paraphrase. "Let me see if I've got this right. You want me to be nothing more than an official figurehead so that you can claim compliance with regulations. Then you can bend the rules to accommodate your freewheeling style. And in return for my compliance, you'll share some of your invaluable, gut-level expertise with me. Is that about it?"

"Pretty much," Grant agreed through a slow, sexy smile that had Caitlin wanting to put her fist right through his pearly white teeth.

Leaning forward so that she was close enough to smell the spearmint on his breath, she tapped him solidly in the middle of his chest. "Mister, you *are* going to take a core sample. Whether you like it or not, my credentials, position, and knowledge give me authority over you. And if I have to shut down this rig to prove it to you, I will!"

Grant guffawed. "You want me to believe that you'd shut down your own daddy's oil rig."

"Just like that," she lied, snapping the fingers of her other hand right in front of his nose.

"You listen to me, honey," he said, dropping his voice to a menacing growl and removing her finger from the bull's-eye which was apparently tattooed on the center of his chest. "A woman can't physically win a pissing contest with a man, and you'd best not forget it."

"Maybe not, *sweetie*," she countered taking equal offense to both the endearment and the crudity. "But a woman certainly is favored in a *thinking* contest."

They glared at one another for the count of ten, neither

willing to be the first to back down. In the stalemate in which they found themselves entrenched, Caitlin hoped Grant didn't call her bluff. As angry as she was at the moment, she would do exactly as she had threatened. And although Grant put little faith in the determination blazing in Caitlin's eyes, he couldn't afford to press his luck. Not with the government. Not with Paddy.

A man of few friends, Grant valued his relationship with Paddy even more than he did the success of their business. Drifting through the shock of his parents' deaths, he had been uprooted when he was sixteen and dumped into his Aunt Edna's home. Seeing to it that he had little time to "idle with the devil," his dear auntie hired him out for every backbreaking job she could find to add to the family coffers. There had been no carefree years filled with the usual high school activities and fun-loving pals for young Grant Davis. No one seemed much inclined to listen to what some wiry orphan with a chip on his shoulder had to say about his future. No one except Paddy Flynn, ironically the man he had initially blamed for his father's death.

Grant had awakened this morning with his mind made up. No bratty college upstart was going to come between him and the man he had come to think of as a father.

"Well," he said, smirking as he popped his gum. "Here comes your *daddy* now. I'll just leave it to you to explain to him why all of a sudden we're going to be so unnecessarily behind schedule."

Caitlin pasted a smile over dry teeth. The last thing she wanted to do was jeopardize her shaky position in the company the first five minutes on the job. She hated Grant for foisting the responsibility of breaking this news to her father. Though she'd never seen it herself, rumor had it that Paddy had a nasty temper when it came to what he considered "tomfool" regulations.

"Everything all right?" he asked, huffing as he topped the last step on the way to the drilling floor.

Slipping an arm through his, Caitlin hastened to assure him, "I was just telling Grant that I'd like to take a—"

"Hold on, darlin'. Before anything else, I want to introduce you to the crew. Why don't you come along with us to the doghouse, Grant?" Paddy asked. "The boys should be up as soon as they finish their breakfast."

Grant nodded his head agreeably and followed them across the drilling floor to the little metal building that housed the crew. Caitlin thought that the term doghouse was an apt name for the stark, utilitarian structure. Decorations inside were limited to bawdy pictures torn from magazines. Finding them highly inappropriate for the workplace, Caitlin wondered just how mad the men would be if their pinups were to suddenly disappear.

Hoping for a professional introduction from her father, one that downplayed their family ties while emphasizing her qualifications, she swept the hat from her head and smiled nervously as Paddy assembled the men. He wrapped a protective arm around his daughter's shoulders.

"I want you all to meet my little girl," he said throwing his chest out pridefully in much the same manner Caitlin imagined he had announced her birth twenty-two years ago. All that was missing was the cigars.

"She's gonna be the on-site geologist for this job, and I want you all to treat her like the lady she is."

Thinking she heard Grant choke behind her, Caitlin resisted the urge to jab her elbow into his ribs.

"That is," Paddy continued, his cheerful bright blue eyes suddenly darkening, "if any of you so much a lay a finger on her, I'll break your arms with a pipe wrench!"

Mortified, Caitlin found herself wishing that the hot blush which engulfed her would reduce her to a little pile of cinders on the spot. She caught a glimpse of Grant out of the corner of her eye. Raising a fist behind her father's back, he silently reinforced Paddy's words. Every man there understood the tacit warning that Grant would back the older man up if the need were to arise. Recognizing the fact that it was his intention to spare Paddy's feelings, Caitlin could think of little else besides her own humiliation. To be championed old-West-style with her nemesis providing backup was almost too much to bear.

Was it so much to ask to be allowed the unencumbered opportunity to earn the crew's respect on her own? It was clear to Caitlin by their resentful scowls that she wouldn't be receiving a genuine warm welcome from any of them soon. Not that she could blame them. Running head-on into a solid wall of family alliance could be painful.

Feeling like the on-site leper, she smiled weakly at them.

"Didn't you have something you wanted to say to your daddy?" Grant prompted.

When she looked at him blankly, he feigned helpfulness. "About a core sample?"

Paddy looked expectantly at her. "What is it, darlin'?"

Resenting the fact that Grant had trapped her into a situation in which she would have to blurt out her intentions in front of the crew without benefit of privately consulting with her father first, she glared daggers at him. If Paddy didn't back her on this, she would be exactly what Grant had predicted—a pretty little puppet.

"I was just telling Grant," she said evenly, "that we need to take a core sample before continuing."

Paddy looked as if she had slapped him with a cold, wet rag. Not only was it cost-prohibitive to stop and pull the pipe when they were in the midst of drilling hole, it would also be necessary to change the drill bit—all of which was time-consuming and labor intensive work. It could shut down the usual flow of operations for up to thirty-six hours. Caitlin was relieved to see that the crew looked far less upset by the change in plans than her father. Then again, they were paid by the hour so deadlines were no skin off their noses.

Paddy started to stammer his protest, but Caitlin shut him down with the proud tilt of her jaw. He rubbed his forehead hard and considered for a moment a number of factors: time, cost, inconvenience—and the feelings his daughter wore so openly on those thick, rolled-up sleeves. When he looked up and realized that the entire crew was watching him as intently as their favorite action movie actor, he barked, "Well, you heard the lady. Best get to it."

Caitlin's heart leapt to her eyes. She shot a triumphant glance at Grant, but her victory was short-lived. The second the last man was out of the doghouse and the three of them were alone, Paddy fixed his eyes upon her with precision accuracy. She squirmed uncomfortably. For the life of her, Caitlin felt six years old all over again—standing before the shards of what was once her mother's favorite heirloom cut glass bowl.

"Just what do you think you're doing?" he demanded.

"My job," she shot back, standing her ground with spine ramrod straight, refusing to allow either her chin or her voice to quiver in front of Grant.

Suddenly the skin around Paddy's eyes crinkled with a proud smile, and Caitlin remembered how her fear of getting a well-deserved spanking all those years ago had been as unfounded as her worry that Paddy would actually undermine her authority in front of the crew. Over a decade ago he had wiped away both his daughter's and wife's tears, explaining how mistakes were nothing more than excellent opportunities for learning. The bowl, he assured his distraught wife, could be replaced far more easily than their daughter's heart.

Paddy turned to Grant with the same matter-of-fact, go-to-it attitude he had instilled in his daughter. "I'll rotate into the schedule today wherever you want me. That way we'll have a better chance of making up the time lost. I'm sure you understand how important it is for Caitlin to establish herself right up front with the crew. I'd really appreciate all the help you can give her. It'd mean a lot to me."

Caitlin was astonished to see all the fight go out of Grant with nothing more than a sincere request for help. Surely he was as worried as she about the strain the extra work would place upon her father. She could not know how Paddy's well-chosen words evoked the memory of a similar show of support for Grant. As a young upstart, Grant had felt the need to prove himself to a driller twice his age and size. By all rights Paddy should have run them both off for brawling on the job. Instead he allowed them to work through their differences on their own—and he took Grant aside to show him some boxing moves he'd perfected in the army. In his prime, Paddy Flynn had been a formidable specimen of manhood.

"Yes, sir," Grant replied solemnly, knowing full well how difficult it was going to be to live up to that pledge.

"And, young lady," Paddy said, turning to speak directly to his daughter. "In the future I'd sure appreciate it if you'd work as a team player."

Caitlin knew better than to try to defend herself at the moment. There would be time enough to discuss it with him later. And with the dirty rat who had deliberately set her atop the horns of a dilemma for the sheer pleasure of seeing her publicly punctured.

"Yes, sir," she replied, resenting the fact that she had just parroted Grant. "In the future I promise to check with you first."

Paddy shook his head. "No, darlin'. Check with Grant, and I'll trust the two of you to do what's best for this company."

With that he took his leave. Like two tigers in a cage eyeing the same piece of meat, Caitlin and Grant considered each other warily. However much they felt betrayed by one another, their allegiance to Paddy was only strengthened by this incident. Caitlin fretted her lower lip between her teeth. When she demanded the core sample, she had had no intention of working her father longer and harder than usual to make up for lost time. That he would willingly do so to keep from compromising her position made her heart swell up like a balloon inside her chest. Oh, what she wouldn't do to be worthy of that good man's approval!

Grant bit back the caustic comment that was on the tip of his tongue. He had given Paddy his word that he would do his best to help Caitlin out, and as much as it rankled him, it appeared he was going to have to play nursemaid to his partner's daughter.

Not that others wouldn't envy him the opportunity. Just as Grant had expected, the leers that lit up some of the crewmen's faces when Caitlin walked through that door spelled nothing but trouble on all fronts. Even baggy coveralls couldn't hide this lady's alluring figure. And that tempting cloud of dark, thick hair simply called out to a man to run his fingers through it and test its softness against his cheek. The only way he could think to keep this little spitfire both safe and productively occupied was to stay as close to her side as possible. To never let her out of his sight if he could help it.

Grant shook his head and sighed. The thought of working with someone who smelled as good as Caitlin presented him with a completely new set of problems.

"Put that hard hat back on, and keep it on," he directed gruffly, wishing there was some way to glue the darn thing to her head. "Apparently it's time to take a core sample."

That he sounded none too happy about it didn't seem to hurt Caitlin's feelings any. Again she narrowed those cat-green eyes of hers at him as she gathered her hair into a loose ponytail and stuffed it beneath the brim of her hat.

Grant wagered that the man who could capture all the sparks in the emerald depths of her eyes could start a forest fire. Feeling suddenly hot himself, he tugged at the neck of his T-shirt as he watched a couple of loose tendrils fall out about her heart-shaped face. Seized by the urge to wind one of them about his finger, Grant had a sudden vision of her naked and willing and—

"Let's get going," he barked, wheeling about on his hard-toed boots and stomping out of the building a good four steps ahead of her.

He could pretty well guess which part of his anatomy Paddy would be coming after with a pipe wrench if he so much as suspected the kind of thoughts his trusted friend was secretly entertaining about his little girl.

Six

By noon Caitlin was forced to abandon her heavy coveralls and strip down to jeans and a T-shirt. Noting how it was modest enough attire for *him* to wear on the job, she chose to ignore the pointed, disapproving stare Grant leveled at her. Even without the hot jumpsuit, she was roasting. The sun overhead had baked a nearby creek bed into great, peeling chunks of clay. Much the way her fair skin was going to look, Caitlin realized, if she didn't take care to slather it several times a day with the sunscreen she had stuck in her back pocket.

Sticky with sweat, she decided that whether Grant Davis liked it or not, she was wearing something cool tomorrow. At this point, a three-piece tailored suit wouldn't make an ounce of difference to the crew. Unaware that she was near enough to overhear, one of the men had said something during lunch break about having to work with *"daddy's little girl."* The other men laughed and leered in her direction.

Caitlin cringed. She couldn't imagine dating let alone being married to such a loathsome creature.

As if it weren't bad enough being despised by her co-workers, Grant had been glued to her all day long like a fly stuck on flypaper. Doubting that he had developed a sudden, overwhelming fondness for her company, Caitlin assumed he was simply afraid to leave her alone for fear that she would either screw things up or simply be unable to fend for herself. Rather than appreciating his attention, she found herself resenting it almost as much as the fact that she was so keenly aware of every bulging muscle beneath the tight white T-shirt he wore. She wished he would have the decency to wear a regular shirt—preferable one three sizes too big with a collar and long sleeves.

Gorgeous body aside, she sternly reminded herself that Grant Davis was indeed the most disagreeable, obstinate man she had ever met. Despite his promise to her father, Caitlin wasn't so sure that he wouldn't deliberately sabotage her efforts just to be rid of her.

"Just shale and sand," she announced with false nonchalance after analyzing the core sample she had insisted they take.

"I could have told you that and saved us all a lot of time, energy, and money." Grant spat the words out as if they tasted as bad as they sounded.

Caitlin squared her shoulders and attempted to hide her chagrin with sarcasm. "Gosh, next time I guess I'll just ask you to walk around, wave your magic witching stick over the hole, and give me your personal take on the situation. That should be enough for me to feel comfortable signing my name as official rig geologist to my reports."

Expecting an equally caustic comeback, she was caught off guard by a reluctant smile that caused something wonderful and uncomfortable to flutter inside her. "Or maybe you could just come with me and check what's coming back up through circulation."

Caitlin tilted her chin at a haughty angle. "That leaves way too much room for costly error."

"You are your father's daughter," Grant remarked enigmatically.

"What do you mean by that?"

"Just that I bet you've never been wrong even once in your life. Paddy's an expert at turning things around to make the other person feel defensive, and it looks like you've inherited the trick yourself."

"I resent that," she retorted, arms akimbo.

And I resent the way your eyes strike sparks whenever I get close enough to see those amazing gold flakes in them, Grant thought to himself. *I resent the fact that it's been so hard for me to keep my mind on my work with you so close at hand, smelling of coconut oil and looking like something out of one of my old adolescent fantasies.*

"The truth hurts," he said offhandedly.

A worry line furrowed his brow as he watched Paddy's struggle to manage the steep walk up the stairs to the doghouse. In his attempt to oversee every aspect of daily operation, he must have been up and down those steps at least a dozen times already.

Caitlin, too, noticed how tired he looked and felt even more guilty about the strain she'd put on her father to accommodate her request for a core sample—especially when it appeared to be, as Grant had predicted, so completely unnecessary. She hated to admit that her father was not as young as he used to be. Though his hair remained thick and his eyes still as bright and clear as the sky above, there was a droop to his shoulders that she had never noticed before. Was she the added burden bowing that once strong back? It had been her intention to lighten his load, not add to it. Caitlin wished there was some way of getting him to cut back a little but at the same time simply couldn't imagine Paddy retired and playing golf every day with those boring duffers who hung out at her mother's country club repeating the same old stories of their glory days. Her father's vitality and zest for life could no more be confined to a putting green than her own considerable energy could be restricted to high society parties where the highlight of the evening was comparing shopping sprees.

Her mother had not realized it until too late to save her marriage. Paddy Flynn was more at home on an oil rig than he could ever be in one of Grandpa Perry's corporate boardrooms. Caitlin liked to think that nothing as comparatively insignificant as the choice of a job or geographical preference could stand in her way if she were ever lucky enough to fall in love with a man even half as wonderful as her father.

"If you could convince him to take a little break with you, I'll relieve Paddy for a spell," Grant suggested.

Accepting the fact that in his mind, Grant would be temporarily rid of two problems at once, Caitlin nodded. By no means was she going to prove a slacker on the job, but there was no reason why she should kill herself off the first day either. It was hot enough to cook a three-course meal on the drill floor, she'd been up and down the steep stairs leading to the doghouse at least fifteen times, and aside from rearranging the heavy equipment in her lab, she had pitched in to help Grant thread some tool joints on the ends of the drill pipe. She put a hand to the small of her back and stretched her muscles. No doubt, she'd be sore tomorrow.

Supper that night consisted of three hungry-man frozen dinners zapped in the microwave. Caitlin promised to get into town no later than the day after tomorrow and pick up some actual, recognizable food. Grateful that all it took to clean up was the rinsing of three forks in the sink and tossing empty containers into the trash, both she and her father opted to turn in early.

After a quick shower, Grant grabbed a blanket from the closet, plopped down on the couch, and tuned in the clearer of the two channels that he could get on their small television set. As much as he would have liked to blame his insomnia on the less-than-comfortable sleeping arrangements, the truth of the matter was his mind wasn't ready to give up his troubles yet. Especially when those troubles came so alluringly packed in five foot six-and-a-half inches of green-eyed, kiss-my-royal-hiney sassiness.

It was late, he was still hot, and television was no panacea for what ailed him. He kicked off his only cover, hoping that enough of a breeze would slip through the window to cool him off. Not a pajama man, he wore nothing but a pair of briefs. He had just switched off the TV when he heard someone padding down the hallway.

Apparently worried about awakening him, Caitlin made her way into the dark kitchen without the aid of electricity. Grant could tell it was her by the lightness of her footsteps even before the soft glow of the refrigerator light revealed her presence. Clad in an oversized T-shirt, she stood in the cool air of the open fridge door. Grant took almost as much pleasure in the fact that she hadn't been able to sleep either as he did in the lovely, virtually transparent view she presented of herself while searching the depths of the fridge.

It came as less of a surprise to him that the thin shirt she was wearing sported the logo of her alma mater's football team than how incredibly sexy he could find such nondescript sleep-wear. As if there had been a doubt before, sleep was out of the question the minute he laid eyes on that young, nubile body showing through her thin nightshirt. His reaction was totally male and totally involuntary as he slipped off the couch and headed toward the light in the other room.

"Looking for a late-night snack?" he asked.

Gasping her surprise, Caitlin banged her head on the open freezer compartment door. She wheeled around to find Grant leaning against the kitchen counter looking rather like a cat with a feather sticking out of its mouth.

"You scared me," she said, rubbing the spot where she'd cracked her head. "How long have you been standing there?"

"Too long for your good—or mine."

Even in the dim light, Caitlin could see the interest glittering in his dark blue eyes. Her tummy tightened, and her heart clattered against her chest like a wild beast rattling its cage. All too aware of the fact that her nipples were as hard as tiny rosebuds, she crossed her arms over her breasts, hoping he would think that the cool air from the open door was the cause.

"Didn't your mother ever teach you that it's rude to go sneaking up on people?" she demanded haughtily. It was all she could do to keep from stealing a peek at that pair of briefs he was wearing. The ones that left nothing to the imagination.

"Didn't yours ever teach you not to go parading around half-naked in front of grown men?"

In less than two steps Grant stifled the indignation sputtering on Caitlin's lips. Crushing his mouth to hers, he meant for the kiss to be punishing. He hoped to put enough scare into this little temptress to either send her running back to Texas or at the very least to keep her safely locked away in the room she had confiscated from him.

Brutal though his intention, the kiss had no such effect upon her. Too surprised to fight against the onslaught of sensations that hit her with the impact of a tidal wave, Caitlin's mind emptied of everything but a warm, accepting fog. She was aware of Grant's hands around her waist like steel bands, making her feel small—but not scared. Despite her innocence, nothing that felt so divine could possibly feel frightening.

Heat suffused her body. Running her hands over a pair of shoulders as wide and solid as a pillar, she was determined to give as good as she got. Since the first moment she laid eyes on him, Caitlin had wondered what it would be like to feel those magnificent muscles beneath her hands, to taste his lips upon hers, to sample the passion glistening in the depths of those phenomenal blue eyes. As each of her senses was assaulted and conquered, Caitlin willingly surrendered herself to him.

Grant made a thorough exploration of her mouth, devouring like a starved man the rich, sensual feast offered him. Caitlin's submissive moans heightened the intensity of his physical reaction. She tasted sweet, so very sweet—like wine and wild flowers and cinnamon. A heady blend of innocence and sinful promises that could easily have a man so tied up in knots it would take the entire National Guard to untangle him.

Not that he was in any hurry to be extricated from such a heavenly embrace. His hands roamed the distance from her small waist, along the sensual length of her rib cage, and came to rest at the sides of her breasts. Caressing their swell with a soft touch made her gasp with pleasure. Caitlin arched her back and pressed her lithe body against his. Grant ground his hips into hers, making sure she understood the extent of his arousal.

Tearing his lips away from hers, he looked deeply into her eyes. They were as wide and full of discovery as a child's on Christmas morning. And just as eager to tear into her first package. Grant was shocked to think that his ploy to scare this little innocent off had just blown up in his face. Beneath the studied coolness towards him that Caitlin wore like a royal mantle was an impassioned woman who like Helen of Troy was capable of launching more trouble than any peaceable kingdom could hope to withstand.

Grant took one giant step backward.

Good grief, what if Paddy were to wake up and discover his darling daughter being ravaged amid the frozen goods? Abused at the hands of the man he treated like a son? Though there was no blood between them, Grant suspected Paddy would feel as betrayed as if there were.

He backed up yet another step and hit the kitchen counter with his backside. Crossing his arms over his heart, he issued a warning.

"You'd best remember, little girl, I'm no wimpy college boy who'll put up with your teasing. Either put some clothes on or stay in your bedroom at night."

The look on her face was of someone who had just been hit in the face with a squirt gun full of cold water. Caitlin wasn't sure whether it was the term *little girl* or *teasing* that wound her arm like up a piston and sent her open hand cracking against Grant's jaw. Quite frankly it didn't much matter. She wasn't about to be kissed, then insulted, all in the span of two shallow breaths.

"If anyone's being a tease, I'd have to say it's you," she snapped in her own defense.

Then with as much dignity as she could muster, she transferred her cold derriere out of the open refrigerator, slammed the door shut behind her, and escaped to the questionable safety of a room permeated by the scent of the first and only man she had ever slapped.

Seven

Just as Grant feared, he was not the only one on the rig to notice their new geologist's decidedly feminine attributes. A pair of khaki shorts and a T-shirt teamed with heavy work boots should have been the furthest thing from provocative, but when Caitlin showed up wearing them the next morning, every head on the drilling floor turned in unison. Any second, Grant expected to see his derrick man come flying out from a hundred feet above. He didn't care how sexist it sounded in this politically correct millennium, a drilling rig just wasn't the place for a pretty woman. A man could get himself killed over a glimpse of those long, shapely legs.

After their heated encounter at the refrigerator, Grant had spent a long, restless night on the couch. Caitlin's well-timed slap had little effect upon the male hormones racing through his body with the force of a mustang coming out of the chute for the first time. It completely boggled his mind how a so-phisticated college graduate with an attitude the size of the

Rocky Mountains could affect such an innocent act all the while kissing him like something out of an X-rated dream.

As long as Caitlin stayed hidden away in the tiny lab located directly behind their trailer, Grant was more than happy to give her all the space she needed. But the instant she stepped outside to check the mud pit and oversee the chemicals used in the drilling process itself, he was all over her like down on a duck.

"I don't need a guardian angel," she huffed, flattening her hands on her hips at his approach.

"The hell you don't!"

The way his eyes traversed the length of her legs made Caitlin feel like she was wearing a slinky skirt with a thigh-length slit rather than a pair of nondescript shorts.

"Does your daddy approve of what you're wearing?" Grant asked.

"My daddy has no more say about what I wear than *you* do," she snapped, her eyes flashing with unconcealed irritation.

"Better cover up," Grant drawled with languid, sexy nonchalance. "If a gentleman like me has a hard time keeping his hands off you in the dark of the night, there's no telling what some of my less refined co-workers might be driven to in the full light of day with so much of your beauty on display."

"You're about as refined as the crude oil we hope is bubbling under this rig."

Fixing him with the emerald drill bits of her eyes, Caitlin tried melting him on the spot with a look of sheer disdain.

He didn't so much as blink.

To her chagrin, Caitlin instead found herself heating up beneath Grant's purely masculine scrutiny. She wasn't sure what to make of that crack about her beauty. Her first reaction was that he was simply making cruel sport of her. When she realized that his eyes held no trace of humor, Caitlin's feminine instincts kicked into high gear. Despite the heat of the day, the mere memory of his hands, his lips, his body pressed against her sent trembles skittering deep in her abdomen.

"How's everything going here?" Paddy asked, wiping the sweat from his brow as he approached. He stopped short to visibly scowl at his daughter's choice of attire.

"Just fine," Caitlin chirped, pointing a finger away from herself to a stack of bags. "I'd like to switch over to this compound and see if it won't improve the stability of the hole."

Paddy grinned as he shot her a mock salute. "Whatever you say."

"Whatever you say," Grant repeated dully.

He noticed that the boss's good-natured humor didn't conceal the pride shining in his eyes. He couldn't help wondering if his father would have shown him the same kind of glowing acceptance—had he but lived to see his son become a man. It was hard not to compare his life with Caitlin's. Although her parents apparently hadn't enough faith in one another to make a go of their marriage vows, they somehow managed to lavish love and affirmations upon their daughter. Grant's own parents had loved each other so deeply that even a mother's love could not keep Cissy Davis tied to the earth once her husband had departed it without her. Within six months of each other, Grant had buried both parents. Adrift in shock for the first year following the double tragedy, he went through the motions of living in alternating states of numbness and anger.

Looking back, his Aunt Edna's cold indifference had been a blessing in disguise. Seeing him as the answer to her own financial worries, she had forced him to put one foot in front of the other, submitting him to a rigorous regime of work without benefit of a heart beating inside of him.

Love had ripped it out and dutifully fed it to the fates.

Since his fondest childhood dream had simply been to have both parents alive and well, it was difficult for Grant to understand what *more* this pampered little princess could possibly want—other than to cut him completely out of her father's heart so she had to share him with no one. The thought knifed him through the chest.

Grant wondered exactly what she was so afraid of. Didn't

she understand that he would do anything in his power for her father? Why would someone graced with so much be so stingy with someone who had so little?

Such a sick, fickle goddess was love that Grant again vowed never to pay her homage. Skin as thick as his could not be pierced by Cupid's arrow. Having every intention to play it safe for the rest of his life, he deliberately limited his involvement with the opposite sex to good times unfettered by demands of any kind. Plenty of women knew the score and were willing to accept whatever Grant chose to give.

Craning her neck to look all the way to the crown of the rig, one hundred and fifty feet above ground, Caitlin broke into his meandering thoughts with an observation. "I can't get over how incredibly big it actually is."

"A little different than the pictures in your college books, isn't it?" Grant sneered.

"I'll say," she agreed, deliberately choosing to ignore the derision in his voice. "I don't think I'll ever get used to the sheer immensity of it."

Grant was right about one thing. An oil rig looked a whole lot less formidable when viewed from a distance.

Throwing a companionable arm around his daughter's shoulders, Paddy shared the breakneck view with her. Against the clear Wyoming sky, Caitlin could almost imagine Jack's giant climbing down this gigantic iron beanstalk from his palace in the clouds. She squeezed her father tightly around the middle and bestowed upon him a dazzling smile.

Grant turned away without saying a word.

He proceeded to throw himself into his work like never before, attempting to chase the long afternoon hours away with the kind of physical labor that taught more than one's muscles a lesson. Immersion in hard work had always been a sure cure for self-pity.

For the first time that he could remember, the strategy failed him.

A stickler for safety, Grant was all too aware that not all of the crew shared his dogged determination to stay focused on the task at hand. All it took to distract the green hand who was catching pipe and loading it onto the beaver slide was the sight of Caitlin below bending over the pipe rack in her shorts. Momentarily fixated on her trim, rounded derriere, Bernie Sommers forgot to pay attention to the speed at which the traveling block was coming down its steel cables.

A ton of steel gave a whole new meaning to the expression "to knock one's block off." The combined roar of all three engines drowned out the warning Grant shouted from below. Nothing makes a person feel more helpless than to watch an impending accident in what seems like slow motion and be able to do nothing whatsoever to stop it from happening. In one brief moment, Grant envisioned Bernie being smacked in the head and being tossed like a rag doll to the hard ground some forty feet below.

Racing across the drilling floor, he tried desperately to get Bernie's attention. Seconds before the moment of impact, the young man glanced up just in time to cover his head with both arms. He desperately tried to sidestep the pipe swinging from the blocks overhead. The glancing blow sounded like brittle wood snapping beneath one's boot as it cracked against his shoulder. Bernie teetered on the edge of the floor, struggling not to lose his balance completely. He would later claim that it was God's hand that pulled him back to safety where he crumpled to the ground in a heap.

Bouncing off the edge of the beaver slide, the pipe careened toward Caitlin. Still bent over her work, she was oblivious to the impending danger. Lungs exploding with the effort of his adrenaline-charged sprint, Grant threw himself at her like a runner charging home plate, knocking her completely off her feet.

The pipe missed them both by inches.

Understanding nothing of his daring rescue, Caitlin knew only that she was being crushed by two hundred twenty-five pounds of solid male. Grant's insinuation that his less than refined co-workers may be dangerous rang in her ears. Fighting her way out of a haze of panic with fingernails bared, Caitlin let out a bloodcurdling scream.

Grant stifled her the surest way that he knew how. Pressing his lips to hers he disarmed her with a mind-numbing kiss. It had the desired effect.

Recognition immediately dawned in her eyes as she gasped his name. "Grant?"

Caitlin felt so incredibly good writhing beneath him and he was so awash with relief to discover that she was all right that he hastened to make her understand what had just occurred before moving his considerable weight off her.

"Let me explain."

"Please do," Caitlin stammered, wondering how she was ever going to get him off her without making even more of a spectacle of herself.

"Keep your head down," he ordered, pulling her so close that she could feel the warmth of his breath on her cheek.

Seeing the pipe dancing wildly above their prone bodies, Caitlin was struck by a blinding flash of the obvious. Understanding replaced fear and confusion in those kaleidoscope eyes of hers.

"My God!" she gasped.

Suddenly grateful for the strong arms wrapped around her, Caitlin felt something behind her eyes go all hot. Trembling, she tried in vain to clasp her hands behind Grant's broad back.

"Shhhh," Grant whispered into her ear. "Everything's all right."

He was only vaguely aware of the flurry of movement about them as Caitlin splayed shaking fingers through his dark hair and pulled his mouth down to hers. To be kissed so thoroughly and so publicly by the boss's daughter was an altogether new experience for Grant. One he knew he should fight like St. George attacking a man-eating dragon, but one he could no more resist than taking the next breath of air. He had done a fair job of convincing himself that the overwhelming physical impact of the kiss he had stolen the previous night had been nothing more than a fluke, but Caitlin's sweet, hungry lips shot that theory all to hell in the span of two thundering heartbeats.

Never before had Grant been kissed with such desperate need. If he could somehow capture the power of this woman's passion, he felt sure the need for fossil fuels would be completely eliminated.

Somebody yelled, "All clear" as Paddy arrived on the scene. Caitlin's piercing scream had brought him flying down that steep flight of stairs two at a time.

The sight of his daughter pinned beneath Grant in the midst of a cacophony of general confusion was enough to put a hurt, bewildered look upon his face. Short of breath, Paddy clutched his left arm with his right, and covered his heart with both.

Hoping the threat of near death would be enough to explain away the questionable position in which he found himself, Grant rolled off Caitlin as quickly as if he had somehow accidentally fallen face first into a bed of hot coals.

"It's all right, Daddy. I'm all right," she hastened to assure him as she jumped to her feet and ran to his side as fast as her wobbly legs would carry her.

But it was too late for explanations as a heart attack brought the big man to his knees.

Eight

"**C**all 911!" Grant yelled, dropping to his knees beside Caitlin to check Paddy's pulse.

Frozen in the terror of the moment, Caitlin was incapable of responding. She was not even aware of her tears hitting her father's chest. The head she cradled in her arms seemed as magnificent to her as that of a downed lion king. Murmuring prayers of divine intercession, she stroked the face that she loved so dearly. His skin felt as cold and clammy to the touch as death itself.

One of the drilling hands raced off in the direction of the cell phone, returning momentarily to report that a helicopter had been dispatched out of Casper, the nearest thing to a city within a hundred miles.

Grant broke into action with a cool head and an eye to the darkening sky. He ordered someone to check on Bernie, called for a stretcher, and helped situate Paddy as gently and surely upon it as if he were actually conscious and aware of every jostling movement. Knowing how dearly every minute counted, Grant decided to move Paddy away from the rig to where the helicopter would land.

Caitlin did not feel the rising wind lash her long, dark hair across her tear-stained face as she held her father's right hand to her heart, trying to transfer her own vitality to him. The wind carried her cries across a sky the color of deep blue velvet.

"Don't die, Daddy."

Grant cupped her face in his hands, peered deeply into her eyes, and commanded her, "Get a grip on yourself."

Having experienced it firsthand at a much younger age, he recognized all the signs of shock. Those exceptional green eyes were glazed and tortured, her face was drained of all color, and she was shivering like a kitten left out in the rain. Grant's firmness could have easily been misconstrued as anger.

"I can't deal with two emergencies *and* your hysterics at the same time. I need your help, Caitlin. So does Paddy."

Shaken by his words from a sense of complete powerlessness, Caitlin mutely nodded her head as she tried to rouse herself from her state of shock.

Positioning four men including himself at the corners of the stretcher, Grant felt a sense of déjà vu. The day of his father's funeral had been overcast and windy. Having insisted on serving as pallbearer, he knew for certain that Keith Davis had weighed far less than Paddy, but the combined burdens of the world could have weighed no more to the sixteen-year-old boy. A half a year later he carried his mother toward the headstone she was to share with her beloved for eternity. Grant had been struck by how very small her white casket looked as it was lowered upon a layer of rose petals that he had placed in that dark hole the evening before when he reached the lonely decision to carry on as best he could on his own, rather than succumbing to the temptation to join his parents in everlastingness.

The anguish in Grant's face mirrored Caitlin's. He did not

think he had the strength to bury *three* parents. Lack of blood ties made Paddy Flynn no less a father to him.

"Don't give up, old man," he commanded the pale man on the stretcher. "Help's on the way."

Embarrassed about causing his own injuries, Bernie refused help as he hobbled down the stairs on his own two feet, cradling his broken arm in his other hand. The unnatural bend was almost as gruesome as the way his shoulder poked through the tatters of a bloody cotton shirt.

It was difficult to pick the helicopter out of the sky, arriving as it did on the heels of dusk amid gathering storm clouds. The time they waited seemed an eternity as the speck on the horizon grew larger and made itself known at last. Dust swirled in a man-made tornado as the 'copter landed in the middle of the sagebrush and the experts rushed into action.

Caitlin tried following the stretcher into the aircraft, but the pilot shook his head. Grant put a gentle, restraining hand upon her arm.

"I'm going along!" she screamed, desperate to be heard over the whir of the blades overhead. "You can't stop me from going!"

The medical technician who strapped Paddy securely in place hollered back. "Sorry, lady, there's only room for one more, and it looks like we've definitely got another patient."

Belatedly remembering Bernie, Caitlin stepped out the way. No matter how desperately she wanted to go with her father, she knew her co-worker's condition warranted immediate attention.

The pilot motioned for Bernie to climb aboard. The young man obliged with a wince and an apologetic glance in Caitlin's direction. Not another word was uttered as the metal bird rose straight up and turned toward a bank of dark clouds. Distant bolts of lightning scissored through a sky bruised purple with the descent of night.

Caitlin said a prayer that her father's heart would soon be beating as rhythmically and solid as the sound of the chopping blades echoing in her ears as she turned in the direction of her vehicle.

The same hand that had held her back from the helicopter detained her once again.

"Where do you think you're going?" Grant demanded.

"To the hospital, of course."

Caitlin's voice sounded hollow and far, far away.

"You're in no condition to drive anywhere." Resisting the urge to gather her into his arms, he employed reason instead. "Besides, you don't even know where you're going."

The reality of that fact slumped Caitlin's narrow shoulders. The myriad of roads that crisscrossed this back country would have baffled Ulysses.

"You take me then," she pleaded. Her eyes were as luminescent as the full moon rising on the horizon so low to the ground that it almost seemed possible to drive right over and touch it.

What Caitlin was asking was impossible. With Paddy and Bernie both out, they were so shorthanded it would be difficult finishing this shift, let alone making the deadline that was going to either make or break the company. Grant understood that compliance with her request would leave but a skeleton crew to manage a hopeless situation. Hell, they might as well start shutting down right now and save the bank the trouble of foreclosing on them.

"Please," she added in a broken whisper.

You're a bigger fool than even I thought possible, Grant told himself as he nodded his head and took the keys from her small, cold hands.

Before taking off, he gathered up the crew and made a brief announcement. "If this wasn't an emergency I wouldn't ask you to make the kind of sacrifices that you'll have to in order to keep this rig up and running until I can get back. You know, of course, that if we can get this rig to pay out before deadline, there'll be bonuses commensurate with your efforts. You have to make up your own minds about whether you're willing to hang in at this point or toss in the towel. I want you to know that I'm not asking for me—I'm asking for Paddy.''

Understanding the seriousness of the situation, the men gathered so somberly about chewed on Grant's words like a tough steak. Tucker Morley broke the silence at last by spitting a long stream of tobacco juice between his steel-toed boots. He turned his withered face to Caitlin and spoke with emotion that cracked his voice.

''I've worked for your daddy in both good times and bad. I don't expect I'll abandon him now. When you see him, do me a favor and tell him not to worry. Old Tuck's got everything under control.''

Tears filled Caitlin's eyes as she hugged the grizzled fellow as tightly as she could. The rest of the crew's assent echoed reassuringly in her ears.

Vowing to be back just as soon as he possibly could, Grant gave them his final orders. ''Just keep on drilling!''

About the time Caitlin's red Jeep pulled away from the site, the rig's photocells kicked in. Illuminated by lights strung the length of the derrick to prevent any low-flying planes from colliding into it, the oil well took on an eerie glow in the motionless silence.

Caitlin appreciated Grant's silence as he negotiated the narrow dirt road. She was in no mood for the empty platitudes of consolation. *God works in mysterious ways… It's far better to go fast than to linger for years in agony… Only the good die young…*

Memories from her past rose up to haunt her. The loveliness of each solitary moment studied in retrospect was as exquisite as sunlight glinting fire off the calm waters where Paddy had helped her reel in her first fish. Or the crimson petals of the dozen roses he'd sent her on the sixteenth birthday when she had felt so certain of her homeliness. Or the softness of the kisses he placed on her cheek when he tucked her into her little white four-poster bed with the gold trim.

''Sleep tight and don't let the bed bugs bite,'' he'd say without fail.

"Sleep tight," she'd repeat before drifting off to sleep blissfully undisturbed by grown-up concerns.

Locked in wordless contemplation with Grant, Caitlin took no comfort as she had as a child in the gentle *swish swish* of the windshield wipers. Tonight they only conjured images of twisted metal tossed from angry skies.

Silent tears streamed down her face like the rain beating against her window.

When Grant reached across the seat to take her hand into his, she did not pull away. Nor did she bother checking the speedometer as they hurtled through the darkness at an average ninety miles an hour. In less than an hour and a half, the lights of Casper winked within their range of vision. Fifteen minutes later they were standing in the hospital lobby being told there was nothing to do but wait patiently until Paddy was out of surgery.

Caitlin was not patient by nature. She placed a call to her mother, urging her to make final peace with her estranged husband. "Before it's too late," she entreated with a broken sob.

The heartfelt request was met by silence and followed with a deep, long sigh. "If it means that much to you, dear, I'll think about it."

"I would think it would mean something to you, Mother," Caitlin chided before hanging up the phone. If a life-and-death emergency could not melt her mother's heart, she didn't know what could.

Unable to contain her anxiety to a sofa and one of the old magazines littering the room, she joined Grant in wearing a path in the nubby beige carpet. Tiring of pacing, he left momentarily to prowl the hospital corridors and returned with two cups of coffee.

Caitlin cradled the cup in her hands and watched the steam curl upward with her prayers.

"Did I ever tell you about the time your old man saved my hide in a little dive outside of Tea Pot Dome?" Grant asked, settling himself beside her on the couch.

Of course he hadn't. Antagonistically positioning themselves for Paddy's favor, they had spent most of their time together doing everything they could to avoid conversation. Up until this very moment it hadn't occurred to either of them to share their mutual affection for the big man who took up so much room in their hearts.

Caitlin found that she was as hungry for Grant's stories as he was eager to tell them. Some were funny, some touching, all illuminated the depth of his love for her father. Regretting that she had initially misjudged him as an opportunist, she listened as he recounted how he had initially blamed Paddy for his father's death.

"And did your mother blame Dad for her husband's death too?" she asked.

"No—she blamed God instead."

The pain of that statement was evident in the shadow that passed over his face.

"Did she ever get over it?"

"I trust she's made her peace with God by now."

During the long pause that followed, Grant's blue eyes turned the color of ice. Caitlin shook her head in confusion. "I don't understand," she said.

"Nobody does," he responded with a hoarse crack in his voice. "My mother loved my father so much that she simply couldn't live without him. If she hadn't taken her own life, I'm sure she would have died of a broken heart."

Caitlin's own heart was rent in two as she came to understand how Grant's gruff exterior hid a horrible hurt buried deep inside him. The possibility of losing her own father beneath a surgeon's scalpel was enough to send tears coursing down her face.

"I can't imagine...I'm so sorry," she said, taking his hand into her own and holding it against her cheek. It felt rough and strong and real. Without thinking, she brought it to her lips and kissed its callused palm.

The sweetness of the gesture loosened something that had been lodged in his heart for years. When Caitlin gently pressed him to continue, Grant found himself talking openly about his past for the first time ever.

"My Aunt Edna was my only living relative. She dutifully took me in, and then proceeded to swindle me out of the Social Security checks I signed over to her with the understanding that they were going into a college fund. No one could believe that such a God-fearing, self-sacrificing woman had secretly spent my money setting up a nice little nest egg for herself."

Caitlin shook her head in disbelief. It was hard to imagine anyone being so cruel to a member of her own family. Since it was bound to remind him of shattered dreams and betrayal, it was little wonder Grant was so bitter every time the issue of her education came up.

"By the time I figured out what she had done, I was a ticking time bomb set to go off. That's when I showed up at Paddy's rig the very day after graduating from high school, blaming him for my father's death and demanding fair compensation for my loss."

Caitlin was amazed to see a grin flicker across Grant's face. "Your father set me straight in short order. Said if I wanted a piece of him I was welcome to try. I didn't know then that he was haunted by his own demons. How some snot-nosed kid couldn't heap any more blame on him than he did himself. I didn't know at the time that the accident cost Paddy his own family. All I knew was that he was actually offering me a chance to make something of myself."

Grant fixed Caitlin with eyes the color of undying loyalty. "I owe your father a whole lot more than my job. I owe him my self-respect and my dignity as a man of my word."

For somebody who prided herself on stalwart behavior, Caitlin felt like a leaky fountain. She wiped her tears away with the back of her hand.

"You have no idea what it means to have you share that with me."

Grant caught one of her errant tears with his thumb and wiped it away. "Your old man's one tough bird," he assured her. "Don't give up on him yet."

Beneath the cold fluorescent lights of the waiting room, they opened hearts long sealed to others' scrutiny and took solace in the swapping of intimate remembrances. When Caitlin broke down in the middle of recounting a rather funny story of how her father had deliberately sabotaged one of her dates to whom he'd taken an immediate dislike, Grant didn't think of the repercussions when he took her into his arms. He just did it.

Caitlin accepted the comfort in the strong arms encircling her, in the sound of the heart beating beneath her ear, in the smell of a shirt stained by honest labor. Without a thought to propriety, she turned her head toward him and offered him her lips.

Their first kiss had been born of passion and anger, the second of fear and relief. This one was delivered of such infinite tenderness that Caitlin was carried away from this frightening, sanitized place on the wings of enchantment. The sensation of Grant's lips upon hers, his hands massaging her spine, his masculine scent permeating her senses was balm to an aching spirit. Caitlin had often wondered what it would be like to kiss this man if she were to actually come to like him.

Now she knew.

It was heaven. As pure and simple as the concept of man and woman.

The feeling transcended time and place. Never before had Caitlin felt so wonderfully protected, so thoroughly cherished as a woman. The tension that had been holding her together melted like butter in the sun. Her muscles grew loose, her limbs heavy as she clung to him in desperation.

Running a hand down the length of her dark hair, Grant stroked her as gently as if he were quieting a frightened colt.

"Get some rest, darling," he whispered, tracing a heart upon one cheek with an index finger. "You need to take care of yourself, too."

Rest was the last thing on Caitlin's mind as her pulse responded to the loving endearment. Certain that the booming of her heart alone was more than enough to keep them both awake through the long night, she allowed herself the luxury of resting her head against the formidable wall of Grant's chest. Smooth and hard, warm and comforting, it symbolized the man himself.

Grant felt her quiver before going lax in his arms.

Unguarded in light, troubled sleep, Caitlin was the most beautiful creature he had ever beheld. Pale and ethereal in the dim light, she looked so vulnerable that his heart lurched with the desire to protect her at all costs. A single word echoed in his brain as he looked upon her.

Mine!

He knew it was nothing short of craziness to allow such a possessive word to creep into his mind. Caitlin Flynn could no more belong to him than he could claim the solar system. Aside from the fact that she was raised in the lap of luxury and educated in the finest schools, she was the daughter of his best friend. A man he had inadvertently put in the hospital.

Assuming that Paddy had believed the worst when he stumbled upon his daughter pinned to the rig floor, Grant held himself responsible for the strain to his heart. If he ever got up out of that hospital bed, he expected Paddy would want to rip his head off. He certainly wouldn't want to entertain any proposals from someone with nothing more than a high school diploma and a stake in a floundering company.

Besides, it was hopeless to wish for anything more than a tentative truce to ever develop between them. And feeling the way he did about Caitlin, friendship was out of the question. He wanted this woman as none other before, and there wasn't a damned thing he could do about it without dishonoring the man they both held above all others.

Grant's arms tightened possessively about her as he allowed his eyelids to drift shut on an intolerable situation.

Sunlight was creeping softly across the tiled floor when he awakened later. The awareness of a sweet heaviness on his chest, foreign and infinitely warm, brought him out of a dream state to the realization that he had somehow dozed off. Look-

ing down upon the woman cuddled up against him, Grant felt
a pang of longing unlike anything he had ever felt before.

*What would it feel like to awaken every day to such a
woman in your arms? To count her as your most precious
belonging? To hold love tangibly against your heart at the
start and the end of your day?*

Caitlin stirred beneath Grant's reflection and sent his
thoughts skittering like leaves on a bonny autumn wind. Long
ago he had come to accept the fact that he was fate's orphan.
Wishful thinking was foolishness, plain and simple. Though
Caitlin's kisses were the closest thing to heaven Grant ever
hoped to experience, they could not erase the differences in
education and background that were certain to come between
them.

A tiny spot of moisture upon his shirt caused Grant to smile.
Certain that such an unladylike indiscretion as dribbling in her
sleep would cause Caitlin enormous embarrassment, he tucked
the endearing detail away in his memory. His mother had once
remarked that what she missed most about her husband was
the small imperfections that had somehow made him completely hers. Before this moment, he had never understood
exactly what she meant.

The sun cast such a rosy halo about Caitlin's hair that Grant
hesitated to disturb it by running a hand over its glossy full-
ness. But like the sailors heeding the mermaid's soulful sere-
nade, he could not resist its magical pull.

Her eyes fluttered open at his touch.

"Good morning, sleepyhead," he said.

"Good morning," she mumbled, snuggling even deeper
into his arms as if it were the most natural thing in the world
to awaken next to him. Her eyelashes grew heavy again for a
blessed moment before they snapped open to reveal the dis-
orientation in their sea-green depths.

"Where?" she stammered. "What time is it?"

Behind them someone cleared her throat.

Caitlin jumped out of Grant's arms like a teenager caught
necking by the local police.

A nurse considered their rumpled state as she approached them. "I understand you arrived here late last night and are awaiting word on Paddy Flynn."

They nodded simultaneously.

"Since he saw no reason to wake you, the doctor told me to tell you that the surgery went well. Mr. Flynn has been moved out of intensive care and is resting now. The doctor will be in later this morning to answer any questions you might have. If you'd like to freshen up in the meantime, we do have a guest bathroom reserved for displaced, out of town family members."

As much as Caitlin wanted to pump the woman for information about her father, she knew the doctor was the one who had the answers. Grimy, gritty, and stiff from a night spent curled up on lounge furniture, she gratefully accepted the nurse's offer.

They followed her to the hospitality room. Not intended for long-term use, it was neither spacious nor luxurious. It did, however, offer clean towels, a few personal hygiene items, and access to a shower. Caitlin went first, mindful to hurry so that Grant would have a chance to clean up as well before the doctor arrived.

They were back in the waiting room within the hour. It was unfortunate that neither one had brought a change of clothes, but a shower did wonders for both their appearance and attitude. With hair still wet, they anxiously awaited word from the doctor.

He showed up a few minutes later, looking red-eyed and weary.

"I take it you're Paddy's daughter?" he asked Caitlin.

Grant cast a protective eye at her as she nodded in affirmation. Frail and frightened, she was on the verge of collapse.

"I'm Doctor Welsh, the surgeon who operated on him." He attempted to stop the questions that flew at him with hands extended outward in a manner reminiscent of a traffic cop. "He's had a heart attack. A serious one. Two arteries were almost completely blocked."

Caitlin clutched Grant's hand and leaned involuntarily into him. Her eyes were hollows of fear.

"He keeps mumbling something about making a bonus good with somebody named Grant. And he wants to see the man immediately."

Looking as if somebody had sucker punched her, Caitlin protested, "There must be some mistake. Surely my father asked to see me as well."

"No, he was very insistent. He wants to see Grant—alone."

Stunned, she looked at Grant through betrayed eyes. Her whole life had been a prolonged attempt to please her father, and in this critical moment, he wanted not her but the son he never had. If Paddy had but a few moments remaining as she was afraid, it seemed sacrilegious to spend them squaring up some damned business deal with Grant—or changing his will so that she was left completely out. Old fears about him being a con man out to swindle her father out of his company reared their ugly heads. The blood pounding in her head apparently was no thicker than water.

"I'm Grant," he said without missing a beat. "What's his room number?"

The doctor hesitated a moment before divulging that information. "I want you to know that this is against my better judgment, but Mr. Flynn is a very persistent man."

This brought a tight smile to Caitlin's lips. If her father were up to fighting the doctors, maybe things weren't as bad as she thought.

"And very weak at the moment. I've got to be honest with you. We've moved him to Intensive Care, but he may not make it through the night. He's asked for a priest as well."

The doctor's words roared in Caitlin's ears like a hurricane beating the coastline. The request for a priest could mean only one thing. Paddy wanted Last Rites administered before he died.

The only thing that kept Caitlin from falling down was Grant's strong arms wrapped about her.

Nine

"I need to talk to you about something important," Paddy croaked, lifting a shaky hand to touch the younger man's arm.

Grant choked back the fear that this place evoked in him. Hospitals always smelled to him of death, and he made a point of avoiding them.

"If it's about the rig, don't worry," he assured his old friend with a convincing lie. "Everything's under control. I don't want you wasting any of your energy fretting about the well not paying off. We're so close to striking oil that I can smell it. And you know my instincts are never wrong."

Paddy's attempt at a smile came out more as a grimace. "My concern is more on a personal level. It's about you—and my daughter."

A muscle leapt in Grant's jaw. Certain that it was the compromising sight of him wrestling Caitlin to the ground that had sent the older man to the hospital in the first place, he was anxious to put Paddy's mind at ease.

"It's not at all what it looked like, sir," he added deferentially. "You have to know that I had no intention of hurting your daughter—ever. It's just that when the pipe swung loose, I—"

"That's not it," Paddy interrupted, vainly trying to lift a hand in the air to brush the offensive assumption away. He swallowed painfully before continuing. "Staring death in the face brings things into focus pretty fast. I realize that there are far more precious things than business to put in order before I cash in my chips. Far too important to be left to chance after my death."

Grant's brow wrinkled in perplexity.

"Sit down, son."

The use of that loving word sapped the strength from Grant's knees and made him glad to reach for a chair. He pulled it up close to the bed.

"I once promised you a bonus for a job well done, and I don't want to go to my maker until I make good on the deal."

Grant shook his head in disbelief. "This is hardly the time to discuss—"

"My time's running out," Paddy rasped. "I've been thinking about how pride stands in the way of a man's dreams. Pride and circumstances."

Reflecting on the circumstances that had taken his parents away from him, Grant nodded in agreement. His heart swelled with love for the remarkable man who had taken him in as a surrogate son. Even without the well paying out, was it possible that Paddy had somehow managed to put aside enough money to help him buy the ranch he had his heart set on?

The very thought brought stinging tears of gratitude to his eyes. It was unbelievable that this man could be so utterly selfless at such a critical time. In light of Paddy's ill health, acquiring his lifelong dream seemed small indeed.

"I'd rather you focus on getting well, Paddy," he said, swallowing against the growing lump in his throat. "I know you're worried about that bonus you've mentioned before, but you don't owe me a thing. It's the other way around."

The tears stinging his eyes were a surprise. Grant hadn't

cried since the day his mother died. When he spoke again, his voice was tight with emotion. "If there's anything I can do to make you happy, just tell me and I'll do everything in my power to make it happen."

The look upon his face left no doubt that he'd move a mountain rock by rock if that what his best friend and mentor wanted him to do.

"I'm glad to hear you say that," Paddy said. Dark clouds of doubt cleared from his eyes as he caught and held Grant in the sincerity of their aging blue depths. "I've watched you change from an angry boy with a chip on his shoulder into a man of character and principle. The kind of man I'd feel comfortable leaving my company to."

Grant's breath caught in his lungs. Such an affirmation was more precious to him than gold. Still the direction this conversation was taking made him extremely uncomfortable. Not only would Caitlin be certain to feel betrayed by her father's dying act of generosity, the plain truth of the matter was that L.L. Drilling would never mean as much to him as to the man who had started it.

As far as Grant was concerned, rig work was just a means to an end, a way of making enough money to buy a pretty piece of land where he could build a real home, one as stable as the one in which he remembered growing up. One not on wheels. Nevertheless the fact that Paddy thought enough of him to even consider bequeathing his company to him was almost more than he could comprehend.

"The kind of man worthy of my daughter's hand in marriage."

So lost was he in his whirling thoughts that Grant imagined he'd heard Paddy offer him his daughter. His lips twisted in wry amusement as he envisioned Caitlin's feminist reaction to such a proposal. Funny what lack of sleep and stress could do to one's mind.

Reining in his stray thoughts with a rough hand, he stammered a bewildered, "What did you say?"

"The two of you were meant for each other. I only wish I

could stick around long enough to see the beautiful children you're bound to have.''

Grant's head snapped up in disbelief. This couldn't possibly be the big ''bonus'' he'd been promised, could it? The tears running down Paddy's cheeks were real enough to convince him that he wasn't just imagining this preposterous invitation to the honorable ranks of the Flynn family.

''Don't you think Caitlin might have something to say about this?'' he stammered incredulously. ''Hasn't she set her sights on a college man, someone with more brains in his head than calluses on his hands?''

''That's just the kind of man she doesn't need. Over the years, I've watched her throw off any number of simpering intellectuals. The truth is I'm worried about her, Grant. When I'm dead and gone, there'll be no one around to protect her from unscrupulous sorts who wouldn't think twice about bedding and wedding a sweet young thing like her for a piece of my business and a permanent address on Easy Street.''

As ''bonuses'' went this one definitely left something to be desired. Grant suspected Caitlin's Twentieth Century convictions would be turned upside down when she discovered she'd been handed over to him as part of some questionable business acquisition. He didn't have the heart to remind his old friend that at the present time his company was not in the best shape it had ever been. They were, in fact, barely holding on. Nonetheless he understood completely Paddy's fear of leaving his only daughter without protection. Outside of the sheltered social circle in which she had been raised, such an innocent would be an easy mark for any number of men. Calculating, brutal men who didn't give a damn about a lady's sensibilities.

The thought sideswiped him and sent his senses spinning out of control. His head began to pound as Paddy continued in a voice that was fast failing.

''Trust me. I've got eyes in my head. I know what my daughter wants, needs, and deserves. You're the best man for the job. Now I'd appreciate it if you'd go get her for me.''

Not willing to put any more strain upon the man he loved

as a father, Grant didn't bother putting up an argument. He stumbled out of Paddy's room looking as if he'd just survived the dropping of the atom bomb.

Still fuming that her father had asked to see him before her, Caitlin regarded Grant with cold fury. He seemed impervious to her anger.

"He wants to talk to you," was all he could manage to say before she pushed her way around him and rushed to her father's bedside.

Tubes, wires, and little plastic bags filled with mysterious fluids sprouted like tentacles in all directions. Looking as pale as the sheets upon which he lay, Paddy appeared already dead. A strangled sob escaped from Caitlin's lips.

"Daddy," she cried, taking a limp hand into her own.

A faint squeeze reassured her as his eyelids fluttered open.

"Cait, you look so pretty," he mumbled. "So like your mother."

The statement was typical of her father. And so sweet and genuine that it caused tears to well up in her eyes.

"You're going to be fine, Daddy. Just fine," she promised, bestowing a kiss upon the weathered hand that had helped guide her though life.

Resting against the pillow, he offered her a weak smile. "I'm glad you're here, honey."

His voice was as unsteady as a reed in the wind, and he looked older than Caitlin could have ever envisioned him. In her mind, her father would be the vibrant man who carried her as a child upon his broad shoulders and allowed her to touch the sky.

"Me, too," she murmured.

"I've asked for a priest."

"But there's no need," Caitlin protested, a note of panic bubbling up in her throat. "I'm telling you that you're going to be just fine. You most certainly are not dying!"

Despite the vehemence of her words, in her heart she wasn't quite so sure. Her father's desire for Last Rites could only mean that he had already accepted the fact that he was going to die. And if that was the case, hope hadn't a chance.

Paddy met her gaze directly. "Yes, honey, I am, and before I go there's something I want to see happen more than anything else in the world."

Caitlin's heart was in her eyes as she fingered the golden locket at her throat. Nestled inside was her most precious belonging: her parents' wedding photograph. Eternally young, they looked lovingly at each another. In times of great stress, Caitlin would revert to her childhood habit of stroking it tenderly. Many a long night she had spent longingly looking at those two happy faces, praying that her parents would somehow get back together. Once upon a time, she had thought that simply wishing upon that amulet could produce miracles.

In the comforting pattern of her old childhood habit, she rubbed the locket between her finger and thumb. "What is it, Daddy?" she asked. "Just tell me; I'll do whatever it takes to make it happen."

In an attempt to make his final wish known, her father strained forward. So as not to tax his voice any further, Caitlin moved even closer.

"A man hates to leave the world with any regrets. I've got one weighing heavy on my conscience that you have the power to remedy."

Caitlin was surprised by the admission. She didn't think her father had any regrets. Anxious to put his mind at ease, she was prepared to assure him that she would do whatever it was he asked of her.

"I've come to rely on Grant like the son I never had. Truth is I couldn't have done it without him. I've been meaning to write him into my will for some time, but I just never got around to it. I don't know how you feel about it, but I'd like to leave half of the company to each of you."

Caitlin had only thought she was too numb to feel any more pain. She was wrong. A pain stabbed through her and left the blade sticking out of her back. Even on his deathbed, her father was more concerned with Grant than he was with his own daughter.

"Like the son I never had…"

Cracking her skull from the inside out, the words rang in her head like a great iron clapper. How fitting. She was to be partners with the man who had stolen her father's affection from her.

"You know I've always felt responsible for his father's death."

Caitlin didn't bother refuting the obvious. This was neither the time nor the place to explain how faulty his logic was. How senseless his guilt was. How misplaced his heart was.

It was enough to know that dear heart was too weak to place any more stress upon it.

Dully, she started to assure him that she would make arrangements to have the proper paperwork drawn up when he stopped her midsentence.

"I've got a better idea. Honey, I've seen the way you and Grant look at each other. Don't even try to deny it. I watched Grant risk his own life to save yours, and I'd feel real good leaving you in his care. I love you both. I just don't have the time to waste waiting for two stubborn, proud kids to work this thing through to its natural conclusion. Maybe it's selfish of me, but what I want more than anything else in this world is to see you married before I'm dead and buried."

Shock registered on Caitlin's face.

"What?" she stammered in disbelief, releasing the locket in her fingers. It burned a hole at the base of her throat as a foreboding tingle raced through her body.

"As your husband, Grant would be automatically entitled to half the company, and I could meet my maker feeling like I'd taken care of you both."

At that very moment a nurse walked through the door with a brusqueness characteristic of a seasoned military man.

"I'm going to have to ask you to leave now," she said, clipping her words sharply.

Indeed Paddy's eyes were already closed.

"Saving his strength is the utmost concern right now," Nurse Ratchet added, ushering Caitlin out the door where Grant was waiting. Though he'd had a few minutes to compose himself, he still looked as shell-shocked as she did. Unfortunately, the hospital corridor offered them little privacy.

They regarded one another warily.

Caitlin broke the silence at last with a question. "Did he tell you what he wants?"

"To see us married before he dies."

"Any chance he was delirious and won't remember a thing that he said?" she ventured.

He snorted derisively in response.

Despite her own bewilderment, Caitlin's pride was wounded by Grant's decided lack of enthusiasm. "Don't worry," she spat out. "I wouldn't dream of asking you to actually go through with it."

"Even if it might mean saving your father's life?" Grant retorted, equally hurt that the prospect of marrying him was clearly so repugnant to her.

A slap in the face would have been less cruel than his words. Caitlin's mouth flew open in outrage at the callousness of the remark.

"You can't actually be considering following through on such a farce!"

Grant's eyes were deep blue drill bits that bore into her very soul. "I'd give my own life for that man," he replied, giving every word deliberate emphasis. "If all it takes is two little words like 'I do' to make him happy, I won't be the one to deny him them."

"But it's ludicrous," Caitlin stuttered. "It's blasphemous."

Still even as her mouth was forming the words, her heart latched onto the possibility of giving her father something to live for. She studied Grant thoughtfully.

"You'd really do that for him?"

His gaze never wavered beneath Caitlin's scrutiny.

"I've seen firsthand what the power of love can do to a person's heart."

Caitlin flinched at the reference to his mother's suicide.

Clearly Grant wasn't willing to risk losing Paddy to a broken heart as well. If granting his friend this small final comfort offered him hope, then his own pride was a mighty small price to pay.

"Need I remind you that we're the cause of your father's heart attack in the first place?"

"No, you don't," Caitlin snapped. As if that knowledge wasn't enough of a burden on her conscience without having Grant add even more weight to it.

He stood before her as solid and immovable as a bronze statue. "I gave him my word," he said, reminding Caitlin of what that meant to a man such as himself.

Sighing, she put her hands to her temples. Her head was throbbing, her knees felt like elastic, and the way the floor was spinning around felt like some persistent child was swatting at the globe of the earth. The only thing keeping Caitlin standing was her concern for her father. She had spent all of her life trying to please him, trying to prove herself worthy of his respect. Hoping to make up for all the precious years she had lost with him, she wanted nothing more than to make him proud and happy—at any cost.

"I suppose that it wouldn't have to be real," she pondered out loud. "As long as we don't consummate the marriage, it could always be annulled later. We could claim to have been pressured under duress or to have irreconcilable differences."

Grant stiffened at her words. He tried tamping the sudden welling of emotion that threatened to betray him. Perhaps being soured on marriage by her own parents' divorce, Caitlin couldn't guess his own secret desire to form the kind of sacred bond that his mother and father had enjoyed. After witnessing the agony that his mother endured at the loss of her husband, Grant had packed those longings away on an icy strand of his heart. Equating love with loss, he preferred his relationships simple and torrid—with no emotional investment.

Unfortunately, he doubted whether Caitlin was the type who could in good conscience buy into such a cold arrangement.

Indeed he wondered whether he himself could remain clinically detached when his blood ran as hot as molten lava whenever she was near. Even now he had to fight the urge to enfold her protectively in his arms and offer her the comfort of his body. She looked so frightened and small against the inevitability of death.

Grant's blood may have run hot, but his words were as cold as an arctic breeze when he spoke again. Never one to deny Paddy what he wanted—much less on his deathbed, he tried to put the situation into perspective.

"Right now our feelings for one another are secondary to your father's wishes. If you're worried that I'm going to force myself upon you and ruin your chances of dissolving our so-called *marriage,* don't be. I promise I'll keep my dirty, working man's hands off you."

His words stung like a bullwhip. No words came out of Caitlin's open mouth. As a befuddled-looking man approached the door checking its number against the one scrawled on the scrap of paper in his hand, she stood gaping like a fish with a hook in its mouth. Dressed in black, the man wore the stiff white collar that identified him to the world as a priest.

He asked the intense, extraordinary-looking couple before him, "Would you happen to know whether this is Paddy Flynn's room?"

Grant indicated that the man was in the right place.

Caitlin held out a shaky hand and introduced herself. "My father is expecting you."

"I'm so glad to meet you at last, Caitlin. I'm Father O'Riley, an old friend of Paddy's," the priest said with a trace of Irish brogue and sincere concern. "I was told it is an emergency."

Taking Caitlin firmly by the elbow, Grant pulled her away from the doorway to allow the priest entry. "I'd appreciate it if you wouldn't rush off, Father. We do need to see you, but right now we've got some pressing business to attend to. I promise we'll be back just as soon as we possibly can."

"That's no problem," the priest assured him with a patient

smile. "I'll pop in on Paddy first and administer Last Rites before making rounds to check on my other parishioners. I'll meet you back here in a couple of hours."

Grant shook his hand with ardent appreciation. "Thank you."

Nodding his head, Father O'Riley checked his watch, opened the door, and went in.

Unable to stand by and watch her father give up on life, Caitlin's voice was devoid of emotion when she addressed Grant again. The words felt thick and awkward in her mouth.

"Can you promise me that this marriage will be in name only?"

Grant's eyes turned the color of blue frost as all hint of gentleness vanished with the onset of bitter winter. "All I want to do is make your father's last hours happy ones. I've given you my word, and it'll have to do. Rest assured, somehow I'll manage to keep my grimy mitts off your lily-white reputation."

It was clear from the scorn in his voice that Grant both questioned her innocence and spurned her pretense. Like so many of the jerks she had dated, he seemed to be under the impression that every girl who went to college automatically lost her virtue with her freshman status. Telling herself that she was perfectly fine with such high-handed assumptions, Caitlin reminded herself that the last thing she needed was Grant's pity. It had been hard enough persuading her college roommate that "saving herself" for marriage was not a joke. Convincing Grant would take physical proof that could be offered but once. And she wasn't about to be goaded into losing such a precious gift by some hard-hat cowboy sporting a chip on his shoulder.

"Come on," Grant muttered, mistaking the pained expression on her face for disdain. "If we're going to do this for your father, we'd better get going."

It was far from the romantic proposal she had so often imagined in her fantasies. Nodding in dry-eyed agreement, she fell into step beside him.

* * *

The next hour and a half passed in a blur. Since there is no waiting period for a marriage license or requirement for a blood test in the state of Wyoming, the necessary paperwork at the courthouse was filled out in no time at all. Signing her name with trembling hand, Caitlin told herself that it was best that there was no time to entertain second thoughts.

On the way back to the hospital Grant pulled into a small shopping center. Caitlin looked at him questioningly.

He nodded in the direction of a mannequin in a storefront window. ''I know it's probably not what you had in mind, but every bride should have a wedding dress.''

Caitlin's heart melted at the sight of the dress the mannequin was wearing. Beautiful in its simplicity, the white sundress with matching jacket was a vision. Delicate embroidery decorated a square neckline, and a sash around the waist was intended to reveal a woman's curves.

Such a feminine outfit was fitting for Southern evenings spent sipping iced tea on a porch swing or nuptials offered in the woods surrounded by wild flowers. The thought of marching into her father's hospital room in the sort of wedding gown her mother had always promised her was just as ludicrous as being married in the pair of shorts she was presently wearing.

Caitlin had to hand it to Grant. He had impeccable taste. The dress was perfect. Not only was it sure to please her father, it also indulged some foolish romantic illusion she had secreted away in some soft spot in her heart. In light of the way Grant was being forced into this farce of a marriage, she couldn't believe his thoughtfulness. Her father was, after all, practically holding a shotgun to his back.

''You don't have to do this,'' she protested weakly.

''If we're going to commit to this idea, we might as well do it right.''

Caitlin's eyes misted with emotion as she swallowed against the tightness in her throat.

They emerged from the mall a short while later. The sundress and jacket fit Caitlin as if it had been custom made for her. She'd also purchased a pair of strappy heels that accentuated the curve of her calves and a very simple veil. Grant looked heartbreakingly handsome in a crisp white dress shirt, silk tie, dark slacks, boots, and new Stetson.

"After all, a man doesn't get married every day," he'd informed the wide-eyed salesgirl batting her eyelashes at him from behind the counter.

Back at the hospital, Grant steered Caitlin toward the gift shop in the lobby and insisted she pick out some flowers for the occasion. Blushing prettily, she chose a small spray of pink roses and baby's breath she hoped would hide her shaking hands throughout the upcoming ceremony.

The gesture made on her behalf was so sweet it made her ache with longing. What girl didn't dream of the perfect wedding?

"Thank you," she murmured, blinking back her tears.

Five minutes later, they were pushing open the door to her father's hospital room.

The faint scent of holy oil lingered in the air. A small white candle by the bedside remained unlit.

"I understand that you two are in a hurry to be married?" the good Father said, quirking an eyebrow in their direction. "Right here and now and in the sight of God."

Caitlin's felt her head bobbing in agreement of its own accord.

"Is that God's honest truth?" he pursued.

"Yes." Grant's single word reply rang as loudly in the room as a death knell.

Father O'Riley regarded them gravely. "It's highly unusual, you know, to perform a marriage ceremony without proper preparation time in which I get to know the young couple first and ascertain whether or not they have a sincere desire to be united forever in the common bond of matrimony. Still, Paddy's an old friend of mine, and he assures me that this is indeed the case. That his precarious condition has merely intensified your eagerness to be wed. Is that truly the case?"

Caitlin looked at her father's closed eyelids. He seemed so

frail and old. Knowing that her answer could indeed be the difference between life and death, she paused but a second before nodding again.

Father O'Riley's voice was solemn. "If either one of you has been coerced into this decision, you must understand that I cannot in good conscience marry you."

Caitlin's voice sounded squeaky from lack of use. "I am choosing this of my free will, Father."

"As am I," Grant said so convincingly that Caitlin found herself wishing he really meant it. That this man truly wanted her to be his wife in every respect.

Paddy sank even deeper into his bed in relief, and a smile as wide as the Rocky Mountains crossed his wizened features. His eyelids fluttered open.

"You look beautiful, Caitlin," he whispered.

Tears welled up in her eyes as she squeezed his hand reassuringly.

"Are you ready to proceed then?" the priest asked, flipping the pages of his worn black missal to the proper place. "As much as I'd like to light a holy candle for a spot of atmosphere, it wouldn't be wise with the patient on oxygen."

The dear Father's desire to romanticize the dreary setting coaxed but a grim smile from Caitlin. She felt strangely removed from the situation, as if watching it from afar.

Surrounded by machines in the stark room, the bride wore white and a bewildered look. The groom sported a rugged look that was far too sexy for such a strained occasion.

It struck her that Grant would look wonderful in the white tux she had once upon a time envisioned for her wedding. It conjured a fetching picture in her mind, one that any number of glossy wedding magazines would have snapped up in an instant. Her husband was indeed the kind of hunk that women swooned over.

Her husband!

Would that he be a husband to her in more than just name! To have and to hold in both sickness and in health...

As much as she would have liked to indulge such fantasies,

Caitlin refused to delude herself. Love played no part in this travesty of a vow. Why, her father might just as well have sold her off to the highest bidder! Being bartered to pay off Paddy's debt of conscience hurt her so deeply that it was all she could do to just stay upright through the ceremony.

There was no ring to put upon her finger, no cake or champagne, no friends to catch her bouquet. All the many loving details a woman puts such stock in were as noticeably absent at Caitlin's wedding as her mother. Her heart twinged with guilt. Laura Leigh would be devastated to discover her only daughter thus married off like a piece of medieval chattel.

As he issued his final instructions, Father O'Reily beamed at Grant. "You may now kiss your bride."

Caitlin stiffened as Grant took her by the shoulders and placed a light kiss upon her lips. They felt as numb as the very soul she had just sold to purchase her father's happiness. Nevertheless she trembled beneath his touch. Considering the circumstances, his tenderness was unexpected and so incredibly gentle that it made her knees buckle. Sagging against Grant's solid chest, she buried her head in the hollow of his shoulder.

Wiping away a tear, Paddy remarked. "I only wish your mother could have been here."

"Me, too, Daddy."

With that Caitlin Flynn Davis bestowed a kiss upon her father's brow, and dropping her voice a notch, whispered into his ear. "Something borrowed…"

Fishing a scrap of lace out of her purse, she slipped one of her mother's scented handkerchiefs behind Paddy's pillow. The familiar scent of honeysuckle wafted through the small room softening the medicinal smell that permeated it.

"You're a darlin' girl," Paddy said.

The old twinkle was back in his eye, and suddenly Caitlin knew Grant had been right all along. Pride and the loss of a cherished childhood dream were nothing in the face of her father's happiness.

Who could it possibly hurt to let Paddy go to his grave thinking his fair line would live on in the passel of grandchildren they had pledged to give him?

Ten

"**Y**ou've done what?"

Caitlin could hardly bear to look at the horrified expression on her mother's face. Though it had been her fondest wish to have Laura Leigh rush to Paddy's bedside, in all actuality she had no expectations that it would come to pass. That her mother had hopped the first plane out of San Antonio at her request only intensified Caitlin's tremendous feelings of guilt for not apprising Laura Leigh ahead of time of her "marriage."

"I refuse to repeat myself, Mother," she replied in a tone that sounded far more petulant than she intended. Still it went against the grain. A married woman should not have to explain herself like some naughty toddler who has just made a mess on the kitchen floor.

Laura Leigh pressed both hands to the sides of her perfectly made-up face as if to keep her head from exploding. In her haste to find Paddy's room, she had virtually collided with her daughter and the brooding, handsome man who was accompanying her. The man's rugged good looks so reminded Laura Leigh of her own first love that it left her tottering on her high heels. No sooner had she regained her footing than the stranger up and introduced himself as her son-in-law. At the pronouncement, the world crumbled beneath Laura Leigh's feet.

Promising to return after picking up a few necessities from a nearby convenience store, Grant excused himself, leaving his bride blushing an explanation.

"Coward," she hissed to his receding backside.

Laura Leigh gave her daughter a baleful look.

"Have you no respect at all for me? For all my dreams of throwing my only daughter a gorgeous, white church wedding the likes of which the entire state of Texas has never seen?"

For one dreadful moment, Caitlin feared her mother was going to burst into tears. Never before had she seen Laura Leigh deal with any emergency with anything less than calming dignity. Dabbing at her eyes with a lacy handkerchief, she was oblivious to the streak of mascara that it left on the side of her aquiline nose.

"I knew I shouldn't have let you come out here to your father's rig," she wailed as much to herself as to her daughter. "I'd hoped to spare you the mistakes I've made in my life."

"I didn't get married just to spite you," Caitlin hastened to assure her mother. Vainly hoping to postpone the inevitable discussion of how this surprising turn of events had come about, she attempted to focus her mother's attention on something other than herself. Caitlin was certain she would stand a better chance against such treacherous weapons as logic and common sense when she wasn't in a state of walking shock.

"I promise I'll explain it all to you later. Don't you want to see Daddy now?" Caitlin's voice cracked with emotion. "It'll mean a lot to him to have you here. It does to me. More than you can know, Mother."

Suddenly Caitlin found herself enfolded in her mother's arms, carried away by the sweet, familiar scent of honeysuckle to those innocent childhood days when a Band-Aid applied with a liberal dose of maternal words of comfort had been a sure cure for any scrape.

"Is he really that bad?" Laura Leigh's voice quavered slightly as a furrow of concern creased her brow.

Caitlin's voice dropped to a shaky whisper. "It doesn't look good. The doctors aren't sure whether he'll even make it."

Her mother's face grew pale. Her lovely mouth quivered, reassuring Caitlin that her feelings for the man had not completely eroded over time.

"Of course I want to see him."

"He was asleep when we left his room. The doctors suggested we get some sleep ourselves and come back later."

Caitlin's voice conveyed her sense of guilt about leaving at all. It had taken all Grant's powers of persuasion to convince her that it was foolish for both of them to spend any more time dozing on a hospital couch.

"Don't worry. I'll be here when he wakes up."

"Are you sure, Mother?"

The questioning look on her daughter's face spurred Laura Leigh into an unwilling explanation. "I've yet to make my peace with your father."

When Caitlin offered to escort her to Paddy's room, the older woman worried her lower lip between her teeth, a sure sign that she was distraught. "No, this is something I have to do myself."

Pausing to take a long look at her daughter's troubled countenance, Laura Leigh's motherly hormones kicked into high gear. "The doctors are right," she concurred. "You look like you're dead on your feet. Go on and get some sleep. I'll stay with your father and call you if anything happens that you should know about."

When Grant returned a short time later, he was surprised to see Caitlin resting her head against her mother's shoulder. Laura Leigh wasn't at all what he had expected. That she had showed up at all was a shocker. That she didn't have two heads and fangs was equally astonishing. In fact, the lady was quite well preserved for her age. That did little to lessen Grant's animosity toward her. Nothing could make him forget that she was the woman who had broken Paddy's heart without a backward glance or a second thought about her wedding vows.

He hoped good looks were the only thing Caitlin inherited from her mother. Despite all evidence to the contrary, he held out a tiny flicker of hope that she might actually consider the vows they had just spoken more than some lines an actress might read from a script.

His own parents had placed the utmost value upon the sanctity of marriage, and he felt certain that the loving bond that connected them in this life remained unbroken in the hereafter. Ashamed of the part he himself had played in that gross burlesque that had just made a mockery of a sacred ritual, Grant made a silent act of contrition. Surely God would forgive him if his intentions were pure.

There was the rub. His intentions were as pure as old Beelzebub's. In the most secret place in his heart, Grant held the desire to do more than simply pretend with his fair bride. A hot-blooded man, he was invariably stirred to arousal by the very sight of her, and playing house was not exactly his style.

As Caitlin stumbled toward him from her mother's arms, bleary-eyed and weak, he reached out to steady her with all protective instincts of a man who claimed this woman as his own.

"Let's get you to bed," he murmured into the sensuous dark waves of her hair, wondering vaguely how he was ever going to bridle his lust once he got her alone.

Grant's comment made Caitlin shiver involuntarily. As much as she would have liked to attribute it to dread, the funny tightening in her tummy made her think twice.

Before she knew it, they were outside the hospital and in the parking lot. Faced with a loveless wedding night on the eve of her father's impending death, Caitlin resisted the urge to laugh hysterically as her husband opened the door of the

Jeep for her. In the face of such bizarre circumstances, his usual chivalry seemed misplaced.

This can't be happening to me, Caitlin thought to herself as she settled herself in her seat and rested her cheek against the cool glass of the window.

"What exactly did you tell your mother?"

Grant's voice sounded raw as he took his own seat and turned the ignition. Having taken a goodly measure of delight in putting a horrified expression on his mother-in-law's face by blurting out that they were married, he couldn't help but wonder if in his absence the two women had shared a laugh at his expense.

"Not much," Caitlin confided with a weary sigh. "I was hoping you could help me out with explanations tomorrow."

Grant reached across the seat and took her hand into his own. It was icy cold to the touch, and he feared she was becoming ill herself.

"Let's get you to a motel," he said.

The tremor he felt go through her hand at the comment signaled his wife's fear of being alone with him in a room with a bed. Instead of setting her mind at ease, Grant focused on navigating the streets of downtown Casper.

With children just back in school and most of their parents working, the streets were relatively vacant save for the rustle of golden leaves and an occasional retiree poking slowly along the dusty sidewalks. Crossing the Platte River's sluggish, murky water reminded Caitlin of just how enigmatic life could be. Like a river meandering through varied terrain, her own days were subject to sudden twists of fate over which she had no more control than the weather.

Her pulse jumped as they pulled into the parking lot of a nice hotel. The thought of registering as Mr. and Mrs. Grant Davis sent all thoughts of desperately needed sleep skittering from her mind like a broken string of pearls hitting a marble floor. Caitlin hoped he had not forgotten the terms of their marriage in such a short time.

It was all she could do to feign composure as Grant approached the desk and returned with but one key. Her mouth flew open in surprise.

"I assumed we'd have separate rooms," she protested. A revealing blush climbed her neck and deposited twin roses upon her cheeks.

Grant pinned her down with his eyes. "You don't have anything to fear from me," he assured her with a derisive twist of his lips. "I've been sleeping on couches for so long the thought of stretching out on a bed all to myself is almost as appealing as sharing one with my lovely bride. The room has two beds, and the truth of the matter is all I want to do is get some sleep."

Unsure of whether it was relief or disappointment that clogged her throat, Caitlin swallowed hard. "I didn't mean to imply that you'd try anything…"

"Don't get me wrong," he added with a glint in his eye that could not be mistaken. "Possessing such a beautiful wife, even in name alone, gives me a great sense of pride. I won't lie to you, Caitlin. I do want you, but I hope you know that I'm not the sort of man who'd force himself on anyone—whatever the circumstances."

"The room then is just…" Caitlin spoke haltingly. "A matter of convenience…like our marriage?"

"Unless you'd like to make it something more."

His words hit her with the force of a blunt object. The look in his eyes was unmistakable. Fearing he would laugh at her if she told him she was a virgin and completely inexperienced at pleasuring a man, Caitlin clamped her lips shut. Whenever a date had begun groping her, she had felt such revulsion to his clumsy advances that she had quickly sent the suitor packing—occasionally amid curses that she was either a tease or a frigid oddball. Those memories clawed at her insides.

What if they were right?

"You don't have to look like I'm leading you to your execution," Grant chided, opening the elevator doors and gesturing for Caitlin to precede him.

Nervousness pricked at the back of her throat as the elevator closed in around them. She felt her stomach drop as the confining box began climbing to its destination. Caitlin feared it had less to do with physics than it did the chemistry bubbling between them. Hoping to steady her nerves, she crowded the far wall of the elevator and concentrated on the changing numbers with each passing floor.

There was no luggage to carry as they stepped off at the appropriate floor, just a small sack of sundries Grant had picked up while she was talking to her mother. A man passing them in the hallway gave her the once-over. Had it not been for the chilling glare she leveled at him, Caitlin was sure he would have winked at Grant in a sleazy sign of brotherhood. The clod seemed to think there was a gross of condoms in the sack she was so nervously crinkling in her hands.

The room was satisfactory on all counts. Dominated by two double beds, it sported a television and heavy drapes that belied the time of day. Caitlin set the sack on the bathroom counter and peeked at its contents. A package of disposable razors, some shaving cream, two toothbrushes, toothpaste, a brush and comb, and a small self-contained cosmetic package soon lined the sink. Grant's thoughtfulness both surprised and touched her.

Who was that crazed-looking woman, so pale and frightened, staring at her from the mirror? Caitlin almost didn't recognize herself. Surely that was no radiant bride reflected in the brutal glare of the glass!

Calling out that she was going to take a shower before hitting the sack, Caitlin set to making herself look and feel better.

"Sure you don't want me to join you?" came his reply through the thin door.

"Positive," she replied in a voice so definitive that it gave no indication that the remark had reduced her mountain of resolve to a mound of quivering gelatin. Snapping the lock on the door, she was chagrined to hear Grant's deep accompanying chuckle.

Cursing him for making her feel childish, she stepped in the shower and let the warmth of pulsating water soothe her jangled nerves. Never had a shower felt so good to her. Knotted muscles gave way to the anticipation of a sexy man awaiting her in the very next room. The image of that man lying in bed wearing nothing but a predatory smile sent a frisson of excitement racing through her. Glad she didn't have to worry about draining all the hot water the way she did back at the rig trailer, Caitlin took her sweet time before emerging from the shower. She wiped the steam from the mirror. Not wanting to look like some painted lady, the tiniest dab of makeup was all that was needed to make her feel a little more confident.

Disinclined toward sleeping in either her soiled clothes or her pretty new sundress, Caitlin wrapped herself in a fluffy towel and put on a brave front. When at last she stepped out of the bathroom, she felt ready to face a firing squad.

Just as she had feared, Grant was sprawled out on one of the beds. Stripped of his shirt, he lay in the glory of a hard-muscled chest. Thankfully, he had retained the modesty of his slacks but had nonetheless unsnapped them causing Caitlin to suck in her breath. Her cheeks were suffused with heat, and a hand demurely covered the panic bubbling on her lips.

A soft snore emanating from the bed relieved her of having to hide her reaction to her husband's masculine virility. Relief and regret did a two-step on her heart as she realized with chagrin that Grant was completely oblivious to the pains she had taken to pretty herself up.

Stepping lightly, she drew the bedspread up over his sleeping form, lingering only momentarily on the tingling warmth of his flesh as she grazed her knuckles across his shoulder. How could such a rough-hewn character look so angelic in his sleep? How could a jaw so rough with stubble beckon so to be caressed? Grant didn't so much as stir, and for that she was grateful. Her breath was shallow as she tucked herself into her own bed. Feeling suddenly chilled, Caitlin pulled the covers up to her chin.

Like some great cat testing its muscles against the new day, Grant awakened gradually. After going so many hours without sleep, his body had demanded its rest. He had succumbed without a fight. Indeed it had been so long since he'd slept on anything other than a lumpy couch that he reveled in long, uninterrupted slumber in the luxury of a firm and spacious mattress. He did not know how much time had passed since he had lain his body down to sleep. Nor was he yet aware of his new bride sleeping not an arm's width away in the next bed.

Feeling safe and secure, he imagined the smell of pancakes and homemade applesauce bubbling on his mother's stove. How he had loved mornings as a child, arising to the happy patter of his parents' conversations, the strong fragrance of freshly brewed coffee, and the expectation that every day was bound to bring wondrous discoveries to light.

Blinking against his memories, Grant opened his eyes to the faint light of dawn leaking through a small gap in the drapes. Disoriented at waking in a strange room, his mind searched for reason in that tender illumination. It took him a moment to realize where he was and to remember that he was not alone. It seemed he was trapped in a fairy tale with Sleeping Beauty.

Leaning on an elbow, Grant took the opportunity to feast his gaze upon Caitlin. She looked so peaceful in her sound slumber that he could not bear to wake her. His guts twisted with longing as he found himself wondering what would it feel like to awaken each and every day with such a woman in his arms.

Heaven, he'd wager.

Hell was being legally married to a woman of such unparalleled beauty and being forbidden to touch her. An orphan with no claim to fame or fortune, Grant didn't expect a woman with Caitlin's sensibilities, social graces, and background to understand that her father had up and given her to him for a job well done. Quite frankly, it was beyond his own understanding.

As temptingly lovely as she was, Caitlin was not exactly the ''bonus'' he had had in mind when Paddy had first made mention of wanting to do something special to compensate him. Grant had expected something quite different for all his years of backbreaking labor and faithful service. Something less primitive than the gift of his employer's only daughter as a mate. Something cold and hard to put in the bank. Something to make the down payment on the ranch he had been dreaming of ever since the day his father had set him in the saddle and walked his pony around the corral.

Grant studied the cascade of hair that spilled across Caitlin's pillow in glorious disarray. She looked quite fetching bundled up in her cocoon of bedding. In contrast to her dark hair, Caitlin's skin was so pale and delicate that it reminded him of an heirloom china doll that his mother had treasured. Placed high on a shelf out of harm's way, the doll would flutter her long eyelashes with a deft twist of the wrist. Oh, how he had longed to touch that forbidden plaything and caress the satin of her gown with rough, little-boy fingers. Like that expensive doll, Caitlin's beauty was reserved for his sense of sight alone. Unfortunately her tousled beauty awoke in him a need so compelling and primal that Grant dared not linger over the sleeping form of his untouchable bride. Having given his word that he would not force himself on her, he was bound to a vow far different than most men take upon their wedding day.

Bitterness clawed at his growling belly as he threw his covers off and headed to the bathroom. Never had Grant imagined starting his honeymoon with an icy cold shower.

Eleven

A freshly shaven Grant looked no worse for wear as he stepped out of his shower. A night of uninterrupted sleep in a real bed seemed to have lifted his spirits considerably. He suggested eating breakfast in the hotel restaurant before heading back to the hospital to check on Paddy.

Eager to put as much distance as she could between herself, her new husband, and their "bridal suite," Caitlin readily agreed. The restaurant was decorated in dark, masculine colors that bespoke country-club elegance. As Caitlin followed a waiter to an out-of-the-way table, it did not escape her notice that all the women in the place twisted their necks to get a better glimpse of Grant's physique as they passed through the room. A fierce possessiveness hitherto unknown to her crept over her. Surprised by the ferocity of the emotion, Caitlin found herself suddenly seized by the need to announce aloud that Grant was *her* husband and that everyone could put their eyeballs back in their sockets.

They both indulged in big breakfasts. Sharing a meal

seemed oddly familiar and comfortable. Through the steam of freshly brewed cappuccino, Caitlin could almost envision sharing a lifetime of such tranquil moments with this man who had pledged himself to her out of sheer love for her father. Her heart swelled with appreciation. Not many men would have acted so selflessly. Precious few would have kept their word about keeping their arrangement chaste.

Caitlin was too worried about her father to linger over breakfast. Soon they were on their way back to the hospital where they found Laura Leigh propped up, half-asleep in a chair beside Paddy's bed. She stirred at the little mewl of relief that escaped Caitlin's lips as she observed the rise and fall of her father's chest with each breath he took. She sank to the edge of his bed with the knowledge that her worst fears had not come true. Paddy had indeed made it through the night.

Laura Leigh arose and put an arm around her daughter.

"He's doing better than they expected, but the doctors say he's not out of the woods yet."

Laura Leigh's once immaculate dress was wrinkled, and dark circles beneath her eyes bespoke what little sleep she had managed during the night. Even bleary, those eyes were as sharp as any scalpel in the place as she turned them upon her daughter.

"You effectively sidestepped me yesterday when I asked for an explanation of why you were married so quickly. I won't be as easily put off today. What exactly is going on here?"

Though Grant stiffened at the inquiry, Caitlin explained in a voice as soft as the beating of her father's heart. "We did it for Daddy."

To Laura Leigh's credit, she did not interrupt once as she listened to the strange tale Caitlin wove. When she got to the part about dissolving their brief, loveless marriage after Paddy was fully recovered and could withstand the news, Laura Leigh pursed her lips and glared at the man on the bed. It appeared Paddy had lapsed back into a sound sleep and was blissfully unaware of the consternation on his ex-wife's face.

Shaking her head in disbelief, Laura Leigh was too much the consummate lady to say more than, "I hope you know how strongly I disapprove."

"It might just save his life, Mother," Caitlin protested.

Grant had been so quiet during their interchange that his deep voice startled both women. "If it does, I'd sure hate to hand him a bankrupt company. Since it doesn't look like there's anything I can do for Paddy here, I'm heading back to the rig. I owe it to him to do everything I can to save the L.L. I'd appreciate it, ma'am, if I could entrust Caitlin to you until I get back."

"Of course, you can," Laura Leigh assured her new son-in-law with an appreciative smile. "I'm not going anywhere for a while."

Rather than being pleased by this turn of events, Caitlin found herself resenting the high-handed way Grant was dumping her. Of course, she reminded herself, that had been his intention since the moment he had laid eyes on her.

"You're going to need me out there," she interjected. "Especially considering how shorthanded we are."

"There's no way I'm taking you back with me," Grant stated unequivocally.

"I can't believe you'd actually want to go," Laura Leigh puzzled aloud.

Years of resentment bubbled over in her daughter's subconscious and found voice. "I'm not like you, Mother. I'm not afraid of the rig or the men or the dangers of the job. I'm not cut out to be the pristine little debutante you've always wanted me to be. Daddy's worked too hard building up this company to let it go to ruin. I won't let that happen without putting up a fight."

"There's no need to stamp your foot at me, dear. You're a grown woman, and you've a right to make your own decisions. If it makes you feel any better about it, I promise I'll stay with your father and keep you both apprised of his condition."

Torn between her loyalty to staying at her father's bedside and her sense of obligation to saving his company, Caitlin felt as brittle as a wishbone. Relief slumped her shoulders. It felt good to be treated by her mother at last as an adult, capable of deciding her own fate.

"Thank you," she said softly.

"Listen," Grant said, running a hand through his thick shock of dark hair in a gesture of extreme frustration. "As much as I appreciate your offer, Caitlin, there's a little matter of propriety to be considered. With your father laid up in the hospital, there won't be anyone to chaperone you at the rig."

"I don't need a chaperone!" Caitlin hotly protested.

"Well, maybe I do," Grant admitted. "Remember it wasn't *my* bright idea to dissolve this marriage by claiming it was never consummated. You'd best remember that I'm no saint, Caitlin."

Neither am I! she wanted to shout at him. Though her face grew hot at the implication of his statement, she refused to be dissuaded from her cause. "We don't even have to tell the crew that we're married," she maintained with such cool resolve that Grant couldn't help admire. "That way you could sleep in the doghouse with the rest of the men, and my reputation could remain chaste."

Grant raised an eyebrow at the sarcastic edge to her voice. "Your reputation may, but you may not. I'd have to go without sleep to keep some sex-starved deviant from trying anything—"

Caitlin's green eyes blazed with indignation. "Don't you think you're overstating the dangers of my staying by myself?"

"No, I don't. Your father would never forgive me if anything were to happen to you."

"Nor would I," Laura Leigh interjected.

Intercepting the grateful look Grant tossed his mother-in-law, Caitlin glowered at them both. Backed into a corner, she nevertheless refused to give up. "Then we'll just have to convince the crew that we're married. Nobody would dare try anything with your wife, and nobody has to know what does or doesn't go on in our little trailer. I'm sure that if you could manage to contain yourself last night at the hotel, you won't have any trouble managing when we're sleeping in separate bedrooms. I'll move into Daddy's room and you can have yours back. You can finally get off the couch and get a good night's sleep."

"With you in the next room? Alone?" Grant wanted to scream. He wondered at Laura Leigh's patience in raising such a headstrong daughter. He doubted whether spankings, time outs, or grounding had ever proven effective with this particular persistent little lady.

"You need me, Grant," she pressed. "You're going to need every bit of manpower we can scrape together. Don't dismiss me just because I'm offering woman power instead."

Grant not only needed her; he wanted her more than she would ever know. But time was wasting while they stood there bickering, and he was not up to the task of arguing such a willful woman out of a position to which she was so obviously committed. Besides, she was right about him needing every available body. If he could just manage to keep his raging hormones under control, she would certainly prove an asset.

"I give up," he admitted with a tired shake of the head. "You win."

Caitlin thought it strange that she didn't feel a sense of triumph at that admission. What she really wanted was for him to *want* her to go with him. That he merely acquiesced to get her off his back was a hollow victory.

Before leaving the hospital they stopped by Bernie's room to see how he was doing. His shoulder and arm were bandaged and in a sling. Considering what damage could have occurred, it was a miracle that only his arm and collarbone were broken. He cocked an eye questioningly at what they were wearing, but neither Grant nor Caitlin offered any explanation for the semiformal attire they had purchased for their "wedding." Glad for their visit and relieved by reassurance that insurance would cover the entire hospital bill, Bernie nonetheless understood their need to cut it short. He was in good spirits when they left him awaiting word from the doctor on a possible early release. He bade them give the crew his regards.

Half an hour later they were on the road again sharing a companionable silence. As he drove, Grant glanced at Caitlin's hands folded so ladylike in her lap. It bothered him to see her ring finger so noticeably naked. Still concerned that some derelict might take a notion to come onto his wife, he was of a mind to put a No Trespassing sign on her ring finger. The knowledge that he was being silly and irrational did nothing to lessen the overwhelming surge of protectiveness he felt.

His mother had left him nothing of value except for her wedding ring. Actually the ring had far more sentimental than monetary value. Flanked on either side by chips, the diamond solitaire itself was pitifully small. Despite its insignificant size, that diamond ring had been his mother's pride and joy. He wondered if Caitlin would laugh in his face if he presented her with such a simple token. The thought made his chest tighten around his heart.

Turning off the main highway onto a dirt road that twisted through miles of uninhabited back country like a snake, Grant was pleased to discover that unlike many outsiders just passing through, Caitlin actually appreciated the unique landscape. Rather than focusing on her fears about her father's health, she marveled out loud at herds of fleet-footed antelope, and saw castles in passing clouds.

Taken in by her imagination, Grant was startled by how quickly time passed. They were at the rig almost before he knew it, and thoughts of how exactly he was going to break the news to the crew that he had married the boss's daughter were suddenly uppermost on his mind. The sight of the small trailer that they were to share under the pretense of a rushed honeymoon sent his imagination racing to forbidden territory.

It had been hard enough containing his desire when Paddy had been there to act as both chaperone and conscience. Without his presence, Grant did not trust himself alone with the woman who had legally pledged herself as his wife. She was such a fascinating creature—part impish sex kitten, part innocent child. And it was that oxymoronic blend of opposing characteristics that left him feeling so completely befuddled.

Unable to imagine anyone who looked as good as Caitlin did surviving the wild collegiate party scene without succumbing to temptation on more than one occasion, Grant felt an unnatural and admittedly unfair lurch of jealousy in the pit of his belly. He suddenly wanted to strangle every zit-faced little preppy who'd ever tried copping a feel from his lovely wife.

Since Caitlin had agreed to go through with the marriage itself, he couldn't help wondering why she had made such a point of keeping their union celibate. Remembering the look of panic that crossed her pretty features when she had broached the subject, he doubted whether it had as much to do with her desire to someday obtain an honest annulment as it did with an aversion to making babies with someone so decidedly beneath her class. Grant's blood boiled as much from anger as desire. In truth, the thought of conceiving a love child with Caitlin sent his mind reeling in forbidden directions. Catching himself daydreaming of dark-haired pixies who resembled their mother, Grant felt a stab of unfathomable regret. To have a ranch where he could find solitude and peace was all he'd ever wanted. In a second, all that was suddenly rendered insufficient.

The longing in his heart would reverberate throughout an empty ranch house.

The instant the Jeep rolled to a stop before the trailer, he outlined his plan. "I'll work straight through the night shift. I figure you'll be able to sleep more comfortably without me around."

Expecting to see Caitlin brighten at the news that he had figured out a way to minimize their contact, Grant was surprised to see a look of disappointment flicker across her face.

After a moment's hesitation, she ventured a surprisingly wifely suggestion. "You're probably hungry by now. I'd be glad to fix you something to eat."

A rueful smile played with the corners of Grant's lips. "Honey, you only have to pretend to be concerned about my welfare when we're in front of the men. I'm perfectly capable of fending for myself. I've been doing it for a long, long time."

Stung, Caitlin wondered if his honeyed endearment was merely a rehearsal for when they had an appreciative audience. Why that silly little word would make her blood throb hot and fast through her veins was not a question she dared to answer just yet.

"Fine," she replied tersely, not wanting to give him the satisfaction of knowing his words held any power over her. She hopped out of the Jeep, not waiting for him to open the door for her as was his usual custom.

To heck with whoever is watching! she thought to herself. *Let them all think our marriage is starting with a spat.*

It certainly wouldn't be out of character. Slamming the door behind her, Caitlin stalked into the trailer.

All the emptiness of the prairie could not compete with the magnitude of the solitude that filled that small trailer. For the first time, Caitlin grasped the full impact of what life might be like without her father. She found herself wandering into his bedroom just to touch his things, just to catch a hint of his aftershave still lingering in the air. Unclasping the locket that she always wore close to her heart, she looked for some sign of reassurance in the familiar faces in that faded, old photograph. The thought of her parents together again after all these years was of some comfort. If they could just keep from killing one another, maybe they could find some special healing for themselves.

Dabbing at the tears that welled up in her eyes, Caitlin told herself to be strong. If they could just make this rig pay out big, she was convinced the good news would provide her father with the will to live.

She slipped out of her clothes, hung the suit neatly in the closet, and changed into clean work clothes. Whether Grant wanted to be around her at all was of no consequence. Caitlin was not here to wallow in self-pity or pander to her husband's whims.

She was here to make miracles happen.

Twelve

"Let's take a short break, sweetheart," Grant suggested, stopping what he was doing to wipe the sweat from his brow with a red handkerchief.

As the crew exchanged meaningful glances, Caitlin blushed furiously to see one man elbow another in the side and surreptitiously mouth the word "nooner." Putting his hand protectively on the small of her back, Grant guided her away from their crude speculations.

As always at his touch, Caitlin was engulfed in sweet flames of desire. It amazed her to see how easily Grant donned the role of a loving husband. Ever since they had arrived back at the rig, tender endearments had tripped off his tongue with unexpected glibness. No matter that they were calculated to deceive an audience, those loving words turned her warm and gushy inside.

Unfortunately Grant's acting ability presented more problems for Caitlin than it solved. Those hot glances he kept sending her way not only convinced the most skeptical among the crew that Grant was utterly smitten, they were also making it almost impossible for Caitlin to concentrate on her job. If he didn't tone it down a notch, she was afraid that she might just accidentally walk right off the drilling rig floor. She knew that marriage was supposed to be a big step, but with forty-some feet to ground level, Caitlin worried that first step could well be her last.

"What is it you want?" she asked, deliberately concealing her irritation in front of the crew by imitating the kind of simpering looks that her girlfriends had donned those numerous occasions when they had fallen hopelessly in love.

"There's something I want to give you."

Taking her by the hand, Grant led her off the floor, down the steps, and toward their trailer. He opened the door for her, but before she had a chance to step inside away from prying eyes, he swept her up in his arms and carried her across the threshold amid the whoops and hollers of their appreciative audience. Squealing in surprise, Caitlin wrapped her arms around his neck and held on tight.

Playacting aside, it felt incredible to be held in a pair of arms as strong as steel, to breathe deeply of Grant's unadulterated masculine scent, and to fall headlong into a pair of crystal blue eyes mirroring the hunger in her own.

Beneath such piercing scrutiny, Caitlin feared her every secret would be exposed. Then again, she reasoned over the pounding of her heart, the fact that she wanted this man as she had never wanted anyone before him was hardly a secret to anyone. Her own father had most certainly known and, in his own indubitable fashion, had taken extraordinary steps to get his little girl whatever she wanted.

She knew only too well how little effort it would take on her part to get caught up in this fantasy, to embrace it heart and soul. In fact, Caitlin would have loved to request in a sultry, sophisticated voice her desire to be carried off to bed and truly wed. Unfortunately the image of bloodstained sheets and the fear of an inept sexual performance on her part blew away her lovely girlish visions with the force of a chilling Wyoming storm.

In college the boys had called her cold and untouchable. Her throat tightened around the memory of one particularly odious frat rat whom she had spurned. He had retaliated by openly pronouncing Caitlin the campus Queen of Ice. She wore the title with a regal, aloof air that belied her hurt.

She pulled the door shut behind them. "You can put me down. Nobody's looking now," she murmured.

Grant looked so disconcerted by the request that Caitlin feared he might just accidentally drop her. But with an aplomb that she was just beginning to expect, he recovered with a charming smile.

"All the better reason not to," he suggested, tightening his grip.

The touch of teasing in his voice didn't quite reach those amazing sky blue eyes as they searched hers for some sign of assent. Finding only hesitation, Grant acquiesced with an exasperated sigh.

To her chagrin, Caitlin's knees buckled the instant he set her down. Feeling suddenly and unaccountably bereft to be standing on her own again, she steadied herself against the solid wall of Grant's chest, longing to rest there forever.

"What do you want?" she asked, her voice an embarrassingly hoarse croak.

The purely masculine look Grant gave her defied her to hear the truth and not back away from it. Unable to maintain contact with eyes that saw too much, Caitlin demurely diverted her gaze.

"Wait here a minute," he ordered, leaving the room.

Caitlin's curiosity was piqued as she heard him shuffling through things in his bedroom. She certainly hoped he wasn't planning to return with some sexual safeguard that would set her cheeks aflame with embarrassment and force her to hotly reiterate the celibate nature of their arrangement.

Grant reappeared a moment later looking far more cautious than she had ever seen him before.

He thrust a small velvet box at her.

"I want you to have this," he said in a tone that struck her as oddly defensive.

Opening the case, Caitlin discovered a wedding ring, a modest diamond of quality cut bordered on either side by matching chips. Taking the ring in her fingers, she was surprised to find it warm to the touch. She could almost feel love and trust emanating from the thin gold band.

"It was my mother's."

"It's lovely." Caitlin was astonished to see his broad shoulders visibly relax.

"I want you to have it."

When Caitlin lifted her eyes to meet his directly, Grant found that the tears glistening in their emerald depths rivaled any earthly jewel, making his humble offering pale in comparison.

"I couldn't possibly accept this. The sentimental value alone—" she began to protest.

"I said I wanted you to have it," Grant interrupted gruffly. He took the ring from her and slipped it easily upon her finger. "I don't want anyone questioning the validity of our marriage. Besides, every bride should have a ring—most certainly one as pretty as you."

Caitlin thought her chest was going to explode. Was it only because she had convinced herself that modern-day chivalry was dead that Grant's gallantry touched her so deeply? Could it be simple coincidence that this particular ring fit as if it had been made especially for her?

Holding it up to the light, she considered its brilliant reflection. "Even brides in trumped-up kinds of marriages that entrap poor unsuspecting bachelors who let their loyalty get in the way of their good sense?" she asked in a tiny voice.

Tipping her chin up with the pad of his thumb, Grant forced her to look directly into his eyes so there would be no mistaking what he was about to say. "Most especially them, darlin'."

His kiss was inevitable. Caitlin tilted her head expectantly and allowed her eyelids to drift shut. She felt Grant's breath, warm and fresh, against her cheek. Slowly he brushed his lips against hers, coaxing them open with expert finesse. His tongue swept inside, plundering the sweetness she had to offer. Waves of liquid heat swept through her, carrying her off to some faraway place where the sensation of Grant's relentless touch was all that mattered.

The moan of pleasure that met each erotic thrust was almost his undoing.

She tasted of ambrosia, he decided. Pure intoxicating ambrosia.

He kissed her until she went limp in his embrace. Reveling in the power he held over her, Grant dragged his mouth from hers to scatter more kisses upon her eyelids, her cheeks, her temples, her earlobes, her long, slender neck before returning once again to concentrate his efforts on lips swollen and pouty.

As a young girl, Caitlin had dreamed of such kisses, yearning for the kind of spiritual transcendence that would leave her breathless and pliant in the arms of some young god. Abandoning all vestiges of resistance, she opened her heart and soul to this wonderful, confounding man who was her husband. The sense of awe that she experienced at the mating of their tongues sent her spinning out of control. She braced herself by wrapping her arms around the strong column of Grant's neck. It was a foundation so solid that she marveled that it could truly be made of flesh and bone. She ran her hands across the expanse of his shoulders and back. Clawing at the thin material of his shirt, she sought desperate reassurance that she was not dreaming.

Despite her frenzied attempts to tear the shirt off his back, Grant continued exploring the delicious secrets of her mouth at his leisure. A moan emitted from somewhere deep inside her as tiny pinpricks of pleasure spread across the surface of her skin. The erotic path his kisses took along the line of her long, slender neck raised goosebumps and made her whimper in helplessness.

Grant gave her no time to consider the matter of modesty

as he unbuttoned her shirt to hastily expose full breasts spilling over the lacy top of her bra. He paused a moment for worship before capturing them ever so gently in his hands.

"You are so beautiful," he murmured, bending his head to place a reverent kiss upon each one.

The world bucked wildly beneath Caitlin. The sight of Grant's dark head nestled between her breasts stirred her to such a fervor that she feared reason would never again return to her. Throwing her head back in silent supplication, she splayed her fingers through the dark thatch of Grant's hair to hold him captive against her heart. Its wild, savage beat stirred in him a primitive reaction.

"I want you," he said simply, raising his head to meet her gaze.

Caitlin's voice was whisper soft. "I want you too."

Only the bravest of women would not have flinched from the feral flame flickering in those eyes of deepest blue. Rising to his full height, Grant issued a velvet warning. "Don't say it if you don't mean it."

Caitlin felt far from courageous as she paused to consider the gift she was offering him. Presenting her virginity to a man who would undoubtedly be surprised by it would surely complicate the deathbed covenant he had made with her father. She knew enough of Grant's character to suspect he would feel obligated to her for life. Obligation born out of pity was the last thing Caitlin wanted from this man.

Such a terrible, wonderful thing is pride that it held her head up at the same time it tore her heart in two. Stepping back, she tugged her blouse shut.

"I do mean it, but we shouldn't forget that..."

She prayed he would not press her for an explanation. Surely he would not force her to admit that somehow mysteriously and against her will and better judgment, she had somehow fallen hopelessly in love with him. Not wanting to offer such a startling admission after rendering her chastity in what may well prove an unsatisfactory performance on her part, she added weakly, "We shouldn't forget that we have an agreement."

Swearing softly, Grant looked at her incredulously. Then, as if to rid himself of the intoxicating effect she had upon him, he shook his head.

Twice.

He wasn't sure what kind of cruel game Caitlin was playing with him, but he doubted she knew how dangerous it was. Few men had the restraint necessary to stop when so obviously aroused. The temptation to take her on the spot was stronger than anything he'd ever felt before in his life. But Grant was gentleman enough to know that when a woman said no, the answer was no.

Even if her body was screaming yes and his was on fire.

Even if the woman was his wife.

It took every ounce of self-control that Grant had to rein in his urge to do what he was longing to do. To make her his in the most elemental fashion.

"Of course. How could I forget our agreement?" he asked with a sneer.

Caitlin felt the lash of his disdain. Unable to defend herself against it, she could not fault his anger. From his perspective, she supposed it might look as if she had purposely led him on. Indeed, rather than stopping his kisses, she had encouraged them. Puffy lips and dazed eyes betrayed her yet. Still aching with desire, her body was a willing accomplice. There was no doubt that physically she wanted him. Insecurity was all that was holding her back. Drawing a hand lightly against his cheek, she tried apologizing in her own fashion with a tender caress.

"Stop it," Grant commanded, grabbing her by the wrist. "I made a promise to you, and I'll do everything in my power to keep it, but I'm only human so, darling, unless you've changed your mind again, I'd suggest you stop giving me mixed signals before I lose all control and do something we'll both regret."

A wave of indecision rocked through Caitlin. She was jealous of the certainty shining in Grant's eyes. He was a man who knew exactly what he wanted and wasn't afraid to grab it.

But would he want her permanently? Rather than engaging in some roll in the hay that was certain to leave her feeling empty and used and ever longing for more, in some old-fashioned part of her being, she secretly hoped the consummation of their union could be the beginning of a real marriage. One entered into willingly by both parties instead of being coerced by her father or out of a sense of guilt over "deflowering" her.

"I didn't mean for... I'm sorry..."

Finding that she could not finish such a lame apology while her body was still tingling from the effects of his hands and lips upon her, Caitlin's words trailed off. She swallowed hard and tried again.

"Considering how you were forced into this marriage, I could only accept your mother's ring with the understanding that you'll get it back when this is over."

"Keep it," he growled as he turned on his heels. "I don't need any more reminders of what a joke marriage is."

She held out her hands to him and called out his name. But it was too late. Grant was already out the door. Its reverberating slam shook the whole trailer.

Caitlin sank to the floor in a puddle of conflicted emotions. The diamond on her hand sparkled in the harsh light. That it had meant so much to the poor woman who had worn it before her was unbearably tragic. The thin gold band made her long for the kind of powerful commitment that could not be severed by even death. The kind that could not be bought by a death-bed wish of a well-meaning father. Or the wishful thinking of a virginal bride.

Diamonds and tears blurred together, jarring in Caitlin's memory a time long ago when her mother had caught her rummaging through her jewelry box. Always lenient about indulging her daughter's penchant for playing dress-up, Laura Leigh had reacted with unusual depth of feeling. In fact, the sight of her wedding ring dangling loosely around her little girl's finger caused her to weep openly.

Only now could Caitlin begin to understand her mother's pain as she tested her own tears against the brilliance of a cold, precious stone. There was no comfort in knowing that she was repeating the same melancholy mistake her mother had made. It seemed she was just as frightened, if not more so, of love than Laura Leigh had been. A pattern of broken hearts could well serve as the family coat of arms. Having always prided herself on being her own person, Caitlin resisted the thought that fate controlled her life.

All these years she had openly resented her mother's faint-heartedness when it came to fighting for the man she loved. Sitting cross-legged on the living room floor in a pool of light streaming through the window, Caitlin came to a decision. If she didn't grab at love with both hands when it was offered to her, it was conceivable that she would die a bitter old virgin regretting the day she let fear rule her heart.

It was time to dry her tears and go after what she wanted.

Thirteen

When the drill bit broke later in the day, Grant thought about volunteering part of his anatomy as a replacement. He had been hard for so long that he thought he would explode if he didn't get some release soon. Hoping to relieve his pent-up frustration, he threw himself into the physical labor required of rig work with a Herculean effort that boded ill for anyone stupid enough to get in his way.

No one did.

Considering how Caitlin and Grant had gotten along before the honeymoon, it came as no surprise to anybody on the crew that the boss's marriage was off to a tempestuous start. When Caitlin showed back up on the drilling floor a couple of hours later bringing her husband a sack lunch, everyone scattered like leaves in the first warning gust of a windstorm. Nobody wanted to be caught in the crossfire of this lovers' quarrel.

Grant was in no mood to see Caitlin. If his body would simply cooperate without collapsing, he planned on working straight through the night shift in a concerted effort to avoid any further contact with his wife. Her last display of bridal jitters had him wound as tightly as a cheap watch. One more deft little feminine twist was all it would take for him to snap.

Hoping Caitlin would get the message, he glared at her as she came sashaying across the floor. The seductive wriggle of her hips had him grinding his teeth in frustration. Like a child baiting a cat with a string, she seemed to take perverse pleasure in dangling her beauty in front of him. The last thing he needed right now was to be reminded of that which was beyond his grasp.

Hurt by her refusal to accept his wedding ring as anything more than a prop in a comic farce, Grant had spent the better part of the last few hours trying to convince himself that it didn't matter. That he didn't give a damn. That years of loneliness had left his heart impervious to such slights. If Aunt Edna's abuse of both his back and his money hadn't taught him not to put his trust in women, he hated to think what it *would* take to make him figure it out. He didn't like to think of himself as stupid, but that was exactly the right term to apply to anyone who thought for a single minute that the high-and-mighty Caitlin Flynn would ever look at him as anything more than oil field trash.

Like mother like daughter, Grant thought scornfully to himself.

Luckily for him, he intended to get out of his "marriage" with his heart and soul intact. Unlike poor Paddy.

The scowl Grant leveled at her did not deter Caitlin.

"I knew you'd be hungry so I brought you a little snack," Caitlin said, presenting her peace offering with a pretty-as-you-please smile pasted on her face. Her tone was so damnably cheery that one might have thought their little altercation earlier had no effect on her whatsoever—had it not been for the telltale puffiness of her eyes that her makeup couldn't completely cover.

He peeked into the brown paper bag she was holding as hesitantly as if there might be a live rattlesnake inside. Flashing a rainbow of colors, sunlight bounced off the diamond on

Caitlin's finger. That she was actually wearing it softened his heart toward her. He had always dreamed that a beautiful, loving woman would someday wear his mother's ring. Of course, Caitlin deserved a bigger diamond to match her fiery nature. Multifaceted to match her many moods and—

Grant's fantasy skidded to a halt. What in the name of heaven was he doing daydreaming about airy-fairy tales and castles in the clouds and happily ever afters? Hadn't Edna beaten such nonsense out of him? He was no more an acceptable groom for such a refined, educated lady as Caitlin than he was a prince on a white charger. The best he could ever hope to offer her would be a mountain ranch that would be a far holler from culture as she knew it.

And the chances of him getting that ranch were growing slimmer with each passing day. If by some miracle Paddy did pull through, he would be sorely disappointed to find that not only were there no grandchildren on the way, the company he'd spent his life building had gone under in his absence.

"I hope you like peanut butter," Caitlin chirped, digging out a sandwich from the bag in her hands. "It was all I could find. If you don't need me this afternoon, I'd like to go into town and pick up some supplies."

I not only need you, I want you—desperately.

"I'm sure we'll manage without you," he replied offhandedly. The truth was the farther away Caitlin stayed from him the better for both of them.

Choosing to ignore the disdain reflected in those steel blue eyes, she asked, "Is there anything special you'd like me to pick up?"

Since living in close proximity with a beautiful woman who acted as skittish as an unbroken colt around him was nothing short of agony, Grant had only one suggestion. "Maybe a chain for your bedroom door."

Caitlin attempted to fight back the blush that rose to her cheeks with unladylike bluntness. "How about a key to my chastity belt instead?"

Grant bit back a laugh and wondered exactly how he had

been tricked into marrying a crazy woman. First she wound him up like a ten-cent top, then cut him off without an explanation. Now she was offering herself to him as a sacrificial virgin. Go figure.

It was enough to make any sane man think about committing himself.

"Save it for someone more gullible than me, honey," he said shaking his head. "I'm not up for any more of your head games."

The next thing Grant knew, he was staring at the world through a blur of peanut butter. Brushing the remains from her hands of the sandwich that she had just smushed into his face, Caitlin turned on her heels and stalked off without saying another word. Despite the peanut butter under her nails, there was nonetheless royal dignity in her bearing.

Grant smiled a sticky smile. He had succeeded in his intent to make her mad. Mad enough perhaps to rent a motel room in town thus relieving him of the pressure of having to endure a sleepless night with her in the next room. Since avoidance clearly was the best strategy for surviving their charade of a marriage, he couldn't quite figure out why his stomach was a churning mass of acid at the thought that he may have accomplished his purpose all too well.

Wiping lunch off his face, he called out after her ramrod straight back. "Thanks for the snack, honey."

Caitlin barely slowed down on her way through Lysite. She was shopping for more than food alone, and the tiny wayside community didn't sport a lingerie shop that she knew of. Unable not to appreciate the irony of her situation, Caitlin considered her plight on the long drive to Riverton, some eighty miles away. All these years she'd been "saving" herself for marriage only to discover that her inexperience was not the advantage her parents had led her to believe.

If anything it was a detriment. Not only was Grant disinclined to believe she was a virgin, she was clueless about how to go about seducing her own husband.

Hurt by his determination to keep as far away from her as possible, Caitlin decided feminine intuition alone would have to overcome both of their doubts about committing to a sexual relationship. Perhaps their marriage was doomed from the start, but she had made up her mind not to emerge from it a freak—the oldest wedded virgin in America.

Remembering the look of appreciation on Grant's face the night she had fixed a simple soup for dinner, she considered the old adage about the way to a man's heart being through his stomach. Arriving in Riverton ninety minutes later, she pulled into the parking lot of a local grocery store where she embarked upon her shopping spree with all the determination of a general drawing up battle plans. She canvassed each aisle for hearty man-pleasing entries, extravagant desserts, and any aphrodisiac that caught her eye. A bottle of champagne completed her purchases. She deposited her groceries in the back of her vehicle and proceeded to a nearby clothing store.

Somehow it seemed to her that the ring on her finger gave her special liberty to linger in the lingerie department. Although Caitlin had indulged in pretty nightgowns, bawdier garments trimmed in black lace and dripping with garters always made her feel uncomfortable. Today she surveyed all the clothing racks with an eye to what her husband might like. Would he prefer her in virginal white? Should she go with the satin midlength in deep royal blue? The sleek Chinese pant set with matching frogs? Or the shocking red teddy that left so little to the imagination?

He'd probably burst into laughter if she came flouncing into his bedroom wearing such a blatantly sexy outfit. The thought propelled Caitlin to put the flimsy teddy back on the rack. If her limited feminine wiles were to be put to the test, she decided it would be best if she did it wearing something that made her feel elegant and alluring rather than simply cheap.

A floor-length gown of diaphanous white made her catch her breath. Except for a few strategically placed satin appliqués, it was all but transparent. Delicate pearl buttons laced all the way up a lacy Victorian collar. Running her fingertips over its satin roses, she felt a feminine twinge deep inside her. Such a flagrantly feminine gown could almost make up for the lack of the white wedding dress she had always dreamed of. She found one in her size and self-consciously set it on the counter.

"Your husband will love this," the saleslady assured her with a conspiratorial wink.

Caitlin ventured a rueful smile of her own as she stared hard at the ring on her finger.

"I'm going to be awfully disappointed if he doesn't," she admitted.

Legally Grant was her husband, and he was undoubtedly the sexiest man she had ever encountered. The thought of seducing him made her blood pump in hot, excited spurts. As the saleswoman rang up her purchase, Caitlin reached for a bottle of perfume, sprayed a dab upon her wrists, and pushed it across the counter.

"Charge this, too," Caitlin said with a smile that fit too tightly across her teeth.

The outrageous cost of her purchases did not discourage her. Price was no object to a woman on a mission.

Grant checked the skyline for what must have been the hundredth time since Caitlin had driven away. It was getting mighty late. Where could she be? Visions of her vehicle breaking down on the side of the road, leaving her at the mercy of unsavory passersby, raced through his mind. Didn't she know that he would worry if she didn't get back before dark?

Ever since she left, Grant had been regretting his hasty words. When she had alluded to the state of her virginity, he had dismissed her claims as being outrageous. He couldn't imagine anyone as lovely as Caitlin surviving high school let alone his idea of the swinging college scene untouched. That he may have misjudged her troubled him deeply. Was it possible that was why she acted so uneasy around him? Not because she found him beneath her, but because she was unsure of herself when it came to her own sexuality? The very thought boggled his mind.

When her Jeep finally pulled into the lot below shortly after dusk, it was all Grant could do to keep from rushing down the rig stairs and wrapping her up in a great big bear hug. Ego, however, kept him rooted to the spot. Once his heartbeat slowed down to a normal range, he planned on talking to her about taking better driving precautions in the wide, open spaces of Wyoming.

As mad as Caitlin had been when she'd stormed off earlier, Grant was astonished to see her look up to the drilling floor, deliberately seek him out, and toss a friendly wave in his direction.

His guts tightened at the mere sight of her. Apparently his lovely wife's shopping spree hadn't been confined to groceries alone. Grant hoped she had alerted the authorities before purchasing the tight-fitting striped jeans and matching knit top that she was wearing. Anything that looked that good from a distance ought to be illegal.

"I'm home, honey," she called up to him in a candied voice.

Oh, what Grant would have given to have wiped that sarcastic grin right off that pretty face with a kiss intended to put her in her place once and for all!

As he stepped through the trailer door a short while later, Grant did a double take as if to make sure certain that he hadn't accidentally stepped into the Twilight Zone. The smells that assailed him were almost as mouthwatering as the sight of Caitlin herself bent over the stove in earnest concentration. The thought of walking up quietly behind her and enveloping her in his arms was more appealing than he liked admitting to himself.

Such was the kind of cozy kitchen scene he'd grown up with. Good food and a loving atmosphere had taken the sting out of poverty. In fact, he hadn't even known how poor his family had been until Aunt Edna hammered the point home by making certain her nephew felt beholden to her for taking in such a destitute relative.

The aroma of pork chops simmering in gravy made Grant's stomach growl. To a man who had cleaned lunch off his face earlier in the day, nothing could have been more filling or satisfying than a hearty meat-and-potatoes dinner. He blinked to see his wobbly little kitchenette table covered with a fancy tablecloth and bathed in candlelight.

"Are we expecting company?" he asked warily. After the peanut butter episode, he was expecting something more akin to all-out war than a peace treaty.

Caught off guard by his sudden presence, Caitlin jumped at the sound of his voice and burned herself on the edge of a hot skillet.

She stuck her fingers in her mouth and mumbled, "No company."

Grant was beside her in an instant.

"Let me see that," he insisted, taking her hand into his and inspecting the damage. Gratified to see that it was but a superficial burn, he nonetheless ordered her to the kitchen sink where he proceeded to run cold tap water over her fingertips.

"It's nothing," she insisted.

"Maybe, but just to be safe let's put a bandage on it anyway."

The diamond on her hand sparkled beneath the cool flow of water all the while her blood boiled beneath the warmth of her husband's concern. Caitlin meekly endured his fussing, feeling rather like a clumsy child who longed to ask her daddy to kiss her boo-boo and make it better.

"There—you're going to be just fine," Grant assured her.

But looking into those emerald eyes glistening with unmistakable feminine interest, he wasn't so sure about his own well-being. Unable to shake the feeling that he was being set up for disappointment again, he released Caitlin's hand and gestured toward the table.

"What's the occasion?" he asked.

"Can't I do something nice without you suspecting an ulterior motive?'' she asked, looking so indignant and domestic in an apron that it caused Grant to throw up his hands in surrender.

"Good point."

"I hope you're hungry," she remarked.

"I am," Grant replied meaningfully. *For you!*

Caitlin couldn't miss the embers of desire glowing in the depths of his penetrating blue gaze. The moment stretched between them humming with the strain of unsatisfied appetites. They were standing so close to one another that when Grant breathed deeply he filled his lungs with the sensual scent Caitlin was wearing.

"It smells good," Grant ventured.

"I hope it tastes good too."

"I'm sure it does."

Those innocent words hung between them like ripe fruit. Suddenly Grant understood exactly how Adam must have felt when Eve offered him that apple.

"I'll just go wash up," he volunteered. Despite his brain's mandate, his feet appeared to be sunk in cement.

The smile Caitlin flashed at him was warm enough to keep their meal hot for hours while Grant did what he really wanted to. His fingers itched to untie the straps of that inexplicably sexy apron, reach for the snap of her jeans, and—

Grant forced himself to remember that Caitlin was offering nothing more than dinner. The "come hither" look in her eyes was probably only the combination of his overactive imagination upon a starving libido. Less than twenty-four hours ago, she had rejected him outright. Only an idiot would read more into the pleasant reception she was giving him this evening. Whether his body agreed or not, it was time to get those wild fantasies he'd been nursing under control pronto.

"In fact, I think I'll get in a quick shower," Grant amended. *An icy cold one!*

An image of silver rivulets of water streaming down his naked body flashed through Caitlin's mind. Hiding her trembling hands in the pockets of her apron, she tried donning the look of an unflustered housewife.

"Fine, that'll give me time to finish setting the table."

Proud of how even her voice sounded, Caitlin turned back to her handiwork bubbling on the stove. Just as determined to serve a perfect meal as she was intent upon sending out all the right signals this evening, Caitlin reminded herself that there would be no turning back for her now.

Love was not for the faint of heart.

The sound of the shower starting in the other room provided her an opportunity to pop the top of the bottle of champagne she'd purchased in town. She regretted the fact that she hadn't thought to buy nice goblets for the occasion as she poured two plastic tumblers full. Bolstering herself with a couple of sips from her own glass, she set the bottle out to breathe.

By the time Grant took his place at the table, Caitlin was feeling a teensy bit bubbly herself.

"Did I hear a gunshot while I was in the shower?" he asked with a puzzled look upon his face.

Giggling, Caitlin pointed out the culprit—the bottle of champagne nestled in a makeshift ice bucket that she had fashioned from an empty coffee can. Her explanation only caused the lines of confusion on Grant's face to deepen. Why had she gone to such trouble to please him? He doubted whether a Ph.D. could figure out this woman's crazy mood swings. He cut into his pork chop, speared a piece with his fork, lifted it to his mouth, and closed his eyes in pleasure. The meat was so tender that chewing was almost optional.

"Delicious," he pronounced, looking straight at the cook.

Caitlin wet her lips with her tongue. "You really like it?" she asked self-consciously.

"I always say what I mean. Don't you?"

"When I know what I want," Caitlin admitted, taking another swallow of her champagne. "Sometimes it just takes me a while to figure that out."

Short of lighting a flare gun, Caitlin didn't know how to give any clearer signals than those she was sending out. Once she had committed to the idea of seducing her husband, it seemed only natural that Grant would buy into the concept, too. Instead he sat across from her, devouring his dinner and looking ready to bolt at any second.

Her mother had always insisted that men liked being the aggressor in relationships. Caitlin had dismissed the idea as being old-fashioned, but in the face of Grant's passivity she had to consider the possibility that Laura Leigh might not be so far off the mark after all. Perhaps she was being too pushy?

The candle on the table flickered against the dark paneling of the kitchen. Like their trust in each another, it struggled to illuminate the shadows in anxious hearts.

"That was fabulous. Let me help you with dishes," Grant offered, pushing himself away from a third helping.

"They'll wait," Caitlin said, hoping he intrinsically understood that *she* couldn't.

"All right then," he said after a moment's pause in which he searched bright green eyes smoldering with unspoken passion. "If you don't mind, I think I'll turn in early."

Those were not the words that Caitlin longed to hear. If eyes burning with the blue flame of desire were any indication, they weren't exactly what Grant really wanted to say either. But having been spurned earlier in the day, he wasn't about to risk his heart again. As Caitlin had so brutally pointed out, they had an agreement, and he was not going to be the one to breach it.

Grant waited for her to detain him.

Caitlin waited for him to make a move.

Any move.

Frozen to the spot, they tried willing each other into movement. It felt as if they were sharing the same breath. They exhaled together.

"Good night then," Caitlin squeaked. The candlelight cast a shadow, making her eyelashes seem as long as butterfly wings. "And sweet dreams."

Illusions. That was the stuff love was made of, Grant thought bitterly to himself. What sweet agony it had been eating the sumptuous meal his beautiful wife had prepared for him. Pretending it could ever be more than an illusion.

Knowing that his dreams were certain to be tortured, he wondered if she meant to mock him with her sweet words.

Caitlin felt the ache in every part of her being as she watched Grant take his gentlemanly leave.

Don't go! she longed to call out, but something painful stuck in her throat. Certain it was pride, she left the dishes in the sink and padded down the hall to her own room, feeling wounded. The negligee she had taken such care to pick out lay upon her bed, a whisper of silken promises. She picked up the beautiful gown and held it against her body. It felt cool and sensuous to the touch.

Pride, Caitlin decided, was a lonely bedfellow.

She stripped out of her jeans and sweater, and quickly slipped the negligee over her head. Reveling in the luxury of satin and silk against bare skin, she studied herself in the mirror. Her figure looked alluring in the clinging gown. Her eyes were wide with passion. Gone was the Queen of Ice. In her place stood a woman ready to embrace her femininity and relinquish her title as the oldest living married virgin in America.

Kicking his covers off in utter frustration, Grant cursed the day he had first laid eyes upon the boss's daughter. That green-eyed temptress of a thousand temperaments had his heart more twisted than the covers tangled about his feet. A breeze whispered through his mind carrying a bewitching fragrance to him, making sleep impossible.

He groaned. Tangible in the air, that intoxicating blend of innocence and jasmine and seduction and musk teased him. Haunted him. Evoking an enchantress to appear in his room. Swathed in white gossamer, she appeared so real to his feverish mind that Grant found himself doubting his sanity.

A voice soft and beckoning wound itself around the very filaments of his being. "I want you," it said quite simply.

Instantly he was alert.

This was no dream. The voice, the scent, the woman bathed in moonlight at the foot of his bed were as real as the beating of his heart.

"What about our agreement?"

Smooth in the darkness, Grant's voice sounded the way whiskey tastes sliding down a parched, tight throat. Burning. Sensual.

"I want to break it. I want to be your wife in more than name alone."

The sight of his muscular body stretched across the bed put a tremble in her knees. He wore only a pair of practical white briefs. Opening his arms wide at the invitation, Grant crucified himself upon the bed, a willing sacrifice to a destiny beyond his control.

Gentle was his tone as he commanded, "Come to me."

Timid was her response as she lifted the hem of her gown and knelt at the foot of his bed.

Caitlin's poor heart was beating so rapidly that she feared it would explode with the strain of her desire to please him in every way. Her fingers fumbled with a pearl button as she struggled to undress seductively.

"Let me help you," Grant coaxed, rising from his prone position on the bed. The gleam in his eyes was primitive. Hungry.

A row of tiny buttons was no match for his impatience as each passing second intensified his building desire. Exposed at last, Caitlin's neck was a lovely thing, as slender and white as a swan's. In the hollow of her throat, a golden locket gleamed in the moonlight. Reverently, she rubbed her fingertips across it.

Seized by the feral desire to replace that cold metal with a mouth both warm and hungry, Grant could endure no more. He placed his hands upon the shoulders of the gown. With a deft movement, the silken garment slid down the length of

Caitlin's bare arms. As soft and dreamy as his most erotic fantasy, it pooled about her knees in shimmering white billows. Aphrodite could have looked no more beautiful as she stepped from the sea foam to undertake the conquest of all men's hearts.

The diaphanous fabric of the negligee provided no protection from eyes that devoured her whole. In an instant, it too was gone, a victim of Grant's skilled fingers. Caitlin quivered beneath his touch. A touch so hot she feared it would singe her skin.

Unable to bear another second of such exquisite torture, she beseeched him to take her. "Please."

Grant needed no further urging. He peeled off his briefs. Naked, he stood before her a conquering warrior.

Caitlin felt no fear, no shame as she lovingly studied her husband's body. The muscles of his broad shoulders and chest gleamed like polished bronze. Pulling her down upon the bed with him, he rolled onto his elbows to keep from crushing her. Caitlin stroked his skin, amazed at its warmth and responsiveness. Goose bumps trailed in the wake of her delicate touch.

Slipping her arms around his neck, she drew him close. His breath was hot and sweet upon her as she pressed her mouth to his. When his tongue parted her lips, she did not fight the intrusion but rather welcomed it by mimicking his actions. Twining her fingers into the hair curling at the nape of his neck, Caitlin arched her back.

Grant grabbed her hips, possessively molding her body to the hard contours of his own. When she tore her mouth from his, he groaned in fear that she was frightened by his strength. Instead Caitlin took his face into her hands and gazed at him with such unconcealed adoration that he could scarcely endure the tender torment of kisses deposited upon his eyelids, the tip of his nose, and the strong, sensitive cords of his neck.

"Caitlin!" he cried out in a voice hoarse with self-restraint.

"Umm?" she responded, not bothering to lift her mouth from the path it had taken along his collarbone and on to the smooth plane of a chest that filled her with awe. She ran her fingertips over its width with a reverence that sent shivers of delight racing through him.

Grant encircled her waist with one arm. His other hand roamed freely over her thighs, breasts, and stomach. His lips claimed her whole body for himself, and when they came to the hardened rosebuds of her nipples, Caitlin cried out in ecstasy as his erotic suckling brought her to the edge of orgasm. At the brink of his own self-control, Grant settled himself between her legs, repeating her name as if it were the most beautiful of prayers. The heat he encountered there pushed him over the edge of all manly discipline as she lifted her hips to his engorged manhood and opened herself to him completely.

"Caitlin!"

He couldn't stop saying her name. Leaning on his elbows to keep from crushing her with his weight, he repeated it worshipfully as he penetrated the most sacred threshold of her being.

Caitlin gasped. The pain of parting with her virginity was brief. Her joy divine as body and soul melded into one. Surrendering herself with a soft moan, she heard her name on his lips grow louder and louder as it built to a crescendo of passion. Simultaneously, they exploded in a white-hot flash of blinding light.

Carried away to a spiritual plane where the visible and invisible came together, a halo of love surrounded them and was suffused in the very breath they shared. Tremors of their lovemaking caused the ground beneath them to undulate. Enveloped in the soft afterglow of intimacy, Caitlin assumed it must have something to do with the world spinning crazily off its axis and aligning itself with the heavenly bodies that preordained long and happy unions. Stars that crossed their paths disintegrated beneath the heat of their passion, leaving but sparkling remnants in her husband's dark blue eyes.

Fourteen

Grant gazed upon the angel in his arms with disbelief. The gift that his beautiful bride had given him was more precious than she could have possibly known. Her innocence was as astonishing as her passion. There was no doubting the blood that proved her claims. Those emerald eyes had been as wide as the moon, her heart as open as the sky when he had entered her and unequivocally made her his. No other woman had ever moved him so deeply, so completely. The honor of being her first was overshadowed by his fierce desire to be her only.

If Caitlin had been scared, she had not shown it. If he had hurt her, she had hidden it well. Rather she had indulged all of his senses in the beauty of making love in a way that he could describe only as reverential. She was the kind of woman every man dreams of possessing—if only for a night.

As much as he wanted to believe in fairy tales, Grant would not allow himself to think this moment could be anything more than fleeting. Once Caitlin awoke to the reality of what she had done, he was certain she would realize it to be a mistake.

It would not be long before she hightailed it back to high society with memories of illicit love with a manual laborer who one night had made her blue blood run red-hot and fast.

Well-acquainted with the harsh facts of life, Grant wouldn't blame her for running. He had learned long ago that shaking his fist at the universe served no good purpose. Such as it was, their lovemaking was a memory he would cherish for the rest of his life. Even though it left him unfit for any other woman, he would be forever grateful to have been in heaven for a single night.

Softly so as not to wake her, Grant ran his hands over her mussed mane of hair. It was a silken veil beneath fingers rough and unworthy. Her whole body was so incredibly soft and curvy that he grew hard again just looking upon her naked slumber. Curling his body around hers, he pulled her even more snugly against him.

Caitlin's eyes flickered open. Stretching like a cat ever so satisfied with her life, she awoke to the sweet pain of having been so well loved. Sighing, she held her hand before her eyes. The diamond on her finger sparkled in the morning sunlight, brightly reminding her that she need feel no guilt for the bruises she cherished deep inside her.

Last night she had been a child. Today she awoke a woman. One who knew exactly what she wanted to do with the rest of her life. Twisting in the magnificent arms that held her, she playfully kissed the tip of Grant's nose.

"I love you," she said simply.

Grant's heart flipped inside his chest like a trout flopping on the banks of his favorite fishing hole. Instinctively distrustful of those sweet words, he reminded himself that such post-sex talk was to be expected of one who has just so recently given up her innocence. Only a fool would make more of it than that.

"Hey there, sleepyhead," he said, cautiously ignoring her unexpected proclamation of love. "How are you feeling this morning?"

Caitlin wrapped her arms around his neck and nuzzled against him. "Wonderful!"

That single word turned to poetry on her lips.

"And hungry," she added. "Ravenous in fact."

"Me too," Grant assured her with a gleam in his eye. "But not for food."

A familiar tingle of pleasure raced through Caitlin's body. Sore though she was, she nonetheless nipped at his earlobe. "Lucky for me you taste as delicious as you smell," she commented with the affected accent of a gourmet French cook.

Breakfast was postponed by another leisurely bout of fabulous, unhurried lovemaking. Satiated and spent, they moved at last from the bed that they shared to the dawn of another day. Caitlin slipped into her robe and slowly adjusted tender muscles to the task of clearing away the dishes left over from the night before. She whistled while she worked, taking enjoyment in the mundane chore. When Grant slipped up behind her and put his hand over hers in an unnecessary attempt to help her break an egg into a glass bowl, she melted against him like the butter bubbling in the skillet she had just set upon the stove.

"Do you have any idea how much pleasure it gives me to make breakfast for my husband?"

Caitlin relished the way the word *husband* rolled off her tongue and settled into her heart. It seemed to her the nature of love to elevate tedious duties so that in the scrambling of eggs and the washing of dirty dishes, one found joy in the providing of humble services. Suddenly nothing sounded lonelier to her than returning to a life of eating alone in posh restaurants, resisting the urge to hide her single status behind some dull literary volume that was supposed to be good for her. A thousand times over, Caitlin preferred sharing a simple meal and a steaming cup of freshly brewed coffee with this man whom she was lucky enough to call her husband.

Grant's heart expanded to the size of a balloon as he watched his wife puttering about their tiny kitchen in a swirl of satin froth. He couldn't help but think how out of place she was here. He wanted to capture every detail of her so that when she grew tired of playing the part of happy trailer-park housewife, she would be indelibly imprinted in his brain. Grant feared that loving aftermath glow in her countenance would all too soon be replaced by more worldly concerns—like how to pay the bills or gloss over her husband's blue-collar roots to friends who were bound to be shocked by her poor conditions.

Caitlin spiced up the fluffy omelet she placed before him with a kiss that almost made him forget his growling stomach.

"Well, what do you think?" she asked, popping a heaping forkful into his mouth and waiting expectantly as he chewed.

"Perfect," he replied with a slow, sexy smile. "And the food's good too."

Made inexplicably happy by the compliment, Caitlin tossed him a saucy look. "Smart man," she commented, feeding him another bite.

They shared the rest of their meal in companionable silence. Already it seemed they were able to read each other's minds in the way that couples who have been married many years do with such unconsidered ease. Caitlin passed Grant the salt and pepper without being asked. He stirred just the right amount of cream into her coffee cup. Neither felt the need to muddle the moment with unnecessary words.

The shrill ringing of the cellular phone on the counter broke their cloistered reverie from the outside world. A feeling of dread came over Caitlin as she imagined the worst possible news about her father. She turned her back to Grant so that he wouldn't see how her hand trembled as she answered the phone.

Left alone to interpret the dainty heaving of her shoulders and her quiet monosyllabic responses, Grant considered whether he should wrap his arms about her now or wait until she got off the phone. Understanding the difficulty of losing both parents himself, he granted his wife the dignity of dealing with her grief in her own way. His own eyes burned red at the thought of losing Paddy. Both of them would need comforting if this phone call confirmed his worst suspicions.

"We'll talk about the annulment later, Mother," Grant heard Caitlin say. His heart grew cold and heavy at the sound of those foreboding words.

The phone was barely settled into its receiver when Caitlin launched herself into his arms. "It looks like Daddy's going to make it after all. He's surprised them all and is making an astonishing recovery!"

"Thank God!" Grant stammered in surprise.

Hopelessly inadequate at putting his own joy into words, he succumbed to the pleasure of having his wife squirm in his lap and tearfully cover his face with kisses. He was certain that life could get no better. Paddy was going to be all right. And Caitlin claimed to love him.

The only dark cloud left on the horizon was the one his dear mother-in-law had brought up. Because of the way she had so heartlessly treated Paddy in the past, Grant couldn't bring himself to care much for the woman. Still, Laura Leigh obviously was no fool. Eager to get her baby out of the farce of a marriage Paddy had foisted upon them, she was certain to enlist all her considerable talent in breaking the union apart. As a woman whose own marriage had failed due to the strain the oil field had put upon it, perhaps his mother-in-law had more right to meddle than he liked to admit.

"I guess since Paddy's out of danger now, your mother wants you to end this little charade," he heard himself say. The words sounded so far away that it seemed the wind had carried them away with the tumbleweeds.

"I told her we'd talk about it later—when we come to town to visit him." Caitlin interrupted herself to drop a kiss upon Grant's furrowed brow. "She's still under the impression that I could get an annulment if I wanted one."

"I don't suppose you told her that's impossible now that we've slept together and I've sullied you."

"Is that what you think you did?" Caitlin asked, jumping

to her feet in indignation. Her voice grew cooler than an air conditioner going full blast at the South Pole. "Sullied me?"

"Isn't that the way your mommy's bound to look at it?"

"I don't give a damn what my mother thinks. I'm asking you what you think," Caitlin exploded. Her face grew ashen as a new possibility entered her brain. "Or is it possible that you think I deliberately went about trapping you into marriage?"

Despite the tension that filled the air between them with charged molecules, Grant smiled at the accusation. "Sweetheart," he said, pulling her roughly back into his lap. "I'm not exactly the sort a privileged rich girl tries to snare. Rest assured the entire world sees you holding the short end of the wedding stick."

The surprise that registered in Caitlin's phenomenal green eyes was almost enough to make him turn from the truth.

Almost.

"You're the one who's bound to feel trapped sooner or later—"

Caitlin put a finger to his mouth in an effort to stop any more deplorable words from coming out.

"Let me finish," Grant ordered, setting his lips in a firm line. He took a deep breath and gave the impression that he was drilling deep inside himself to find just the right words.

"There's an old saying," he began. "When poverty knocks at the door, love flies out the window. I may not like the fact that your mother doesn't think I'm good enough for you, the truth of the matter is, Caitlin, you deserve a better man than one who can offer you nothing more than the sweat off his back. A back in the process of being broken in half," he added, thinking of the likely fate of L.L. Drilling Corp.

Grant felt every muscle in his wife's body tense. Rather than being placated by such painful honesty on his part, Caitlin looked hurt.

"Do you really believe that I'm so shallow?" she asked.

"God knows that I wish the rest of my life could be like last night. Unfortunately as nice as it sounds, we can't spend the rest of our days in bed. Whether you want to admit it or not, the truth of the matter is that we come from real different backgrounds, darlin'. I was raised on elk meat and flour gravy. I suspect you dined on gourmet cuisine.''

"So what?'' Caitlin asked in a burst of petulance. "I don't see how what we ate as children has anything to do with the here and now.''

"Believe me, it does. I suspect that you'd tire of wild game pretty darn fast. I also happen to think that it wouldn't be fair to ask you to live a life so far beneath what you're used to. I can no more see you living from paycheck to paycheck than I can imagine you on your knees scrubbing out toilets. And the sad fact of the matter is, the likelihood of me being able to hire a maid any time soon is as about as good as us striking oil while we're sitting here trying to change the sorry state of the world.''

This rather long speech on his part was met by dead silence. Caitlin did not stir from her position in his lap. Sitting ramrod-straight, she did not move so much as a muscle.

Grant rubbed a hand over his morning stubble and tried dislodging a lump the size of a baseball that was stuck in his throat.

"All I'm saying is that you might be better off doing as your mother suggests and just forgetting about me. You're going to want to pursue a new life back in Texas once this project—and this marriage is over.''

"Sorry to disappoint you,'' she said, gripping him by the shoulders as if trying to drag him from a raging river. "If you think you can brush me off after sleeping with me for just one night, you can just forget it. I have every intention of sleeping with you for a lifetime.''

Moist with unshed tears, her eyes were luminous jewels, emeralds shot through with the fire of defiance. Grant loved the stubborn way his wife stuck out her lovely chin when she was determined to have her way. Placing a kiss there he murmured, "That's a lovely thought, but I won't hold you to it, sweetheart.''

Caitlin refused to be dissuaded by the funny feeling in her tummy that his endearment evoked. "Just in case you're not sure what I'm trying to say, let me clarify. Whether you like it or not, you're stuck with me, cowboy."

"The only thing either of us is stuck with is an unreasonable deadline and a promise to your father to keep his company afloat—at least until his heart is strong enough to withstand the news that his company is likely to go belly-up."

"You mean bankrupt?" Caitlin gasped, slumping into a kitchen chair of her own.

At the horrified expression on her face, Grant realized his mistake. He swore softly under his breath. He should have expected that Paddy would protect his daughter from the worst.

"You didn't know?" he asked.

"Only that things have been better in the oil business and that he has his hopes pinned on this particular rig." Caitlin's face was ashen, her voice reed thin. "I had no idea it was that serious."

"Don't worry," Grant said, laying a comforting hand upon her shoulder. "Paddy's sure to have protected your assets."

Hurt that he would think her concerned only for herself, Caitlin replied dryly, "The amount of credit you give me is overwhelming." Jumping to her feet, she began to pace in agitation. "How long do we have?"

"Less than two weeks."

"Two weeks?" she groaned in disbelief. No wonder Grant had been so upset about taking the time to do that core sample she had insisted upon. No wonder her father had been pushing himself so hard.

"We'd better get to work then," Caitlin declared, dismissing the morning's dishes with a critical eye.

Grant didn't have the heart to tell her it looked hopeless. In the best of circumstances, the oil business was a crapshoot. What with Paddy laid up and them being shorthanded, their chances of salvaging the company in two weeks were next to nothing.

Two weeks was barely time for a woman of privilege to truly consider the implications of living from hand to mouth. Barring any miracles, when the company went bust, Grant would be just another in a long line of out-of-work oil field hands looking for a job. He was sure that Laura Leigh could relate horror stories of what life was like beating a trail between rigs in the extremes of Wyoming's unpredictable weather.

"You can sit here in defeat if you want," Caitlin declared, interrupting his somber musings. "But I'm not about to give up without a fight."

With that, she swept out of the room in a swish of satin that stirred the scent of perfume left lingering in the wake of her sudden departure. Grant shook his head at his wife's determination. He supposed she planned on using the same magic to save her daddy's company that she employed in turning him from a frog to a prince.

The sound of someone pounding at the front door so startled him that Grant almost spilled his coffee. Since the only time any of the men came calling was to deliver bad news, it didn't bode well.

"That's probably poverty I hear knocking at my door," Grant said cynically to the dregs in his coffee cup, "telling me that the honeymoon's all but over."

Fifteen

"Boss, you gotta minute?"

Don Schaunders stood in the doorway of the trailer with his hands in his pockets, maintaining eye contact with the top of his steel-toed boots. "I think you'd better come to the floor."

One glance at the lost look on his relief driller's unshaven face assured Grant that whatever awaited him was not favorable news. A dozen possibilities raced through his mind. None of them conjured up any pleasant images.

"Tell me what happened," he commanded.

"Looks like we're stuck in the hole."

"Let me put on my boots, and I'll be right there," Grant assured him. "Don't do anything until I get there."

Having already been designated as the official whipping boy, Don was relieved to discover that the boss wasn't particularly interested in looking for someone to blame. Instead Grant preferred assessing the situation himself.

Everyone knew the timing couldn't have been any worse. How unfair for fate to add yet another weight to a bar already bent beneath its heavy load of trouble. A superhero would have difficulty bench-pressing any more bad news.

Making their deadline under optimal circumstances had been a long shot in the first place, but Paddy was a consummate gambler who thrived on such challenges. And Paddy wasn't here to buoy their flagging spirits. Shorthanded, everybody was exhausted and out of sorts. Add to that disastrous combination the fact that the boss had up and married the owner's daughter, a wet-behind-the-ears geologist determined to do everything by the book, and you got a crew that was confused, fatigued, and a little suspicious. Between an unexpected honeymoon and what appeared to be an impending divorce, they worried whether Grant was capable of handling yet another emergency.

Not a man among them was unaware of the dangers of working with someone who couldn't keep his mind on business. Several were missing fingers from similar experiences. Others had witnessed firsthand the untimely death of fellow crewmen on other rigs. Poor Bernie who had been rushed to the hospital along with Paddy was just another example of what happens when a man's concentration wanders from the perilous task at hand.

Tugging on the laces of his boots, Grant knew he had to move fast to get whatever the problem was fixed with minimal delay. Their shoestring budget was seriously frayed, and they simply could not afford any lag in work. The truth of the matter was it wasn't just an expensive drill bit stuck in that hellhole. It was the entire future of the company.

Grant called out to Caitlin who was in the process of getting into her work clothes in the back bedroom. "I'll meet you on the drill floor as soon as you get dressed. It seems we have yet another crisis, and I could probably use your opinion."

Slamming on his hard hat, he wasted no time getting there himself. Caitlin was right on his heels. They both arrived to find everybody standing around, looking anxious, and waiting for further instructions.

Because they were shorthanded, the mud man had attempted

to cover two jobs. While filling in for the missing floor hand, he had neglected to keep a close enough eye on the circulation material, and the mud had gotten too thin. The result was much like pouring water into a mound of sugar. A portion of the hole had caved in around the drill bit.

To say that they were stuck was an understatement. Over twenty thousand feet below them, the bit was sealed so tightly in its tomb that all the pressure the blocks could pull were unable to budge it an inch. If it was anything like being buried alive beneath a mountain of debt and misgivings, Grant knew the feeling only too well.

"What do you think?" he asked Caitlin. "Anything in the last core sample that could shine some light on our current predicament?"

"It doesn't look good," she said, trying her best to keep her voice level so as not to give way to panic. "A combination of sand and shale probably caused the hole to collapse. My suggestion is to cut the pipe above the bit with an explosive charge, pull out the pipe, and fish the bit out. If we get right on it, we could be back in business before you know it."

Caitlin added that last sentence to cover the doubts dragging her heart to her toes. Proper procedure and regulations demanded no less than what she was recommending. The time required was a luxury they could ill afford, but to her knowledge there was no way of getting around it. It seemed all their hard work was destined to crumble beneath circumstances beyond anyone's control.

"I have a better idea," Grant said.

Caitlin could almost hear his mind shifting into high gear. The resignation in her eyes was suddenly replaced by a glimmer of hope.

"We're going to pump some oil straight down to the bottom of this hole and see if we can't lubricate the bit enough to drill up through what's caved in. It's a bit unconventional, but the way I see it—"

"A bit unconventional!" Caitlin interrupted, almost choking on the word. "It's not only unconventional—it's insane."

She felt compelled to remind him that one of the rudimentary principles of drilling was that it was done with a carefully controlled combination of water, mud, and chemicals. Despite the lowly connotation his name might imply, the mud man in charge of maintaining the proper mixture for the changing conditions was highly respected in the business for his expertise. What Grant was proposing was little more than a childish regression to making mud pies far below the surface of the earth.

Determined to stand her ground on this issue, Caitlin placed her feet shoulder width apart. "From everything I've read—"

"Sweetheart," Grant interrupted.

The word that had been intended to mollify had the exact opposite effect upon Caitlin who hotly resented being patronized before the crew.

"Yes, darling?" she hissed.

"There's a whole lot more to the oil business than what you read in books. There's experience and intuition and—"

"And utter nonsense!"

Trying to compose herself after this outburst, Caitlin continued in a more solemn, self-possessed manner. "Nobody wants this rig to pay out more than I do. For God's sake, its failure could mean a relapse for my father. But no matter how important it is to the success of this company, Daddy wouldn't ever deliberately—"

Unable to stand the censure in those dazzling green eyes a second longer, it was Grant's turn to interrupt. "And just who do you think taught me this little trick? None other than your precious daddy himself. And if he were here right now, that's exactly what he would do under these circumstances."

Duly reminded both of her inexperience and the fact that Grant knew her father far better than she did, Caitlin glared at her husband through a haze of tears that she absolutely forbade to fall in public. Though her mother had always maintained that a thin line separated love and hate, until this very moment, Caitlin hadn't known just how slender that thread was.

In a flash of insight she understood that it was not an issue of background, money, or education that doomed their marriage. Their differences went far deeper than comparisons of elk meat and flour gravy to Veal Cordon Bleu. It struck Caitlin as ironic that Grant was actually the snob he accused her of being. His contempt for her credentials was as ingrained as his resentment of her past. A past of pampered privilege which he pictured without thought to her childhood loneliness or the obstacles she had faced in obtaining her geology degree over her mother's, grandparents', and all of "polite" society's objections.

Marriage to Grant was bound to be a collision of his experience pitted against her education. With sudden certainty, Caitlin doubted whether he could ever accept her as an equal in this marriage.

And she could accept no less.

"It appears there's nothing I can say to change your mind," she said, trying hard to look and sound impassive. "You're going to do whatever you want anyway, aren't you?"

Aware that she was referring to more than just his decision on how to best proceed with this particular problem, Grant met her steady gaze directly.

"Yes, I am," he admitted. "As much as I appreciate your opinion, Caitlin, I'm still the boss around here, and we just don't have the time to do this by the book."

Seeing the look of defeat upon her lovely face, Grant longed to take his wife into his arms and reassure her that everything would work out all right. Just as he had seen his own father do for his mother countless times before. Unfortunately when things hadn't worked out as promised, Cissy hadn't been able to cope.

"Schoolbooks don't have all the answers, Caitlin. And neither do I. But after working my way up in the business from the bottom up, I've developed a nose for oil. Call it a gut feeling. Call it instinct. Call it whatever you like. I'm telling you, we're so close to hitting oil that I can almost smell it."

Afraid that it was desperation that he smelled, Caitlin was tempted to assuage her hurt feelings by stalking off and leaving him to manage without her help. Unfortunately knowing only too well the constraints under which they were all laboring, she could hardly expect the crew to remain by Grant's side if his own wife were to walk out on him at such a critical time. She felt forced to abide by her husband's decision, if only out of loyalty to her father.

"Then I suggest you tell me what I can do to help and we'll see about getting this show on the road," she said, biting the words off in crisp syllables.

The look of surprise that crossed Grant's face was quickly replaced by a flicker of pride in his clear blue eyes. The courage and determination his pretty wife displayed in the face of impending doom was daunting. He had expected her to abandon him—just as every other woman had at the most critical times of his life. That she would acquiesce so meekly to having her opinion overridden before the crew was almost as astonishing to Grant as the fact that she was made of sterner stuff than either of their mothers, both of whom chose escape when life got hard.

Caitlin was her father's daughter as well—and so much like him that it caused a smile to hover about Grant's lips. Acknowledging the sacrifice to his wife's pride with a slight nod of his head, he began issuing directives. As the crew scurried off in all different directions, he turned to Caitlin, allowing her a glimpse of tender gratitude glowing in his eyes.

"Thanks for your support. I appreciate your sticking around to help," he added.

"I'll stay as long as you need me," she replied.

I need you for the rest of my life, Grant longed to admit, but before he could, the first barrel of oil arrived and with it a flurry of activity that pushed personal considerations aside.

As much as Caitlin would have loved to feign disinterest, her curiosity was piqued by the proceedings. She watched in fascination as they poured the first of the full barrels of oil into a container that would pump it into the drill string. Unused to the strain being required of them, the mud pumps started up with a growl.

"Stand back!" Grant ordered.

"What can I do to help?" Caitlin demanded, wary of being pushed aside in an effort to protect her. Unless there was a damned good reason for her to go, she was determined to stand beside her husband. Right up until the bitter end.

"I need you to see if we've got circulation yet. Go down to the mud pit and see what Joe needs help with."

Although she knew Grant was trying to protect her from a hazardous situation, the request was reasonable enough to force Caitlin's compliance. The truth of the matter was, her services would be more valuable to the mud man right about now than on the drilling floor itself. As she headed down the stairs, she heard her husband yell to his driller.

"Donny, put some pressure on this pipe and try to get it turning."

The intrepid driller did as he was told, gradually increasing pressure at Grant's command. A short while later when the rig began to creak beneath the strain of the blocks, Grant immediately ran over to relieve Donny of his duties. "I'll take over from here," he said in a tone that breached no discussion.

Suddenly the whole rig shook, and the earth emitted a low growl as the bit popped loose like a tooth being extracted from the mouth of some terrible giant.

Even from her safe spot far below at the mud pit Caitlin could hear the crew's jubilant cheers. She checked her watch. It was unbelievable. Barely an hour had passed since Grant had made the decision to bypass her recommendation and do things his way. Undaunted by her dire predictions that it couldn't be done, Grant had shown her it could. And far from being offended at being proven wrong, Caitlin was delighted. Although their chances of striking oil before the deadline passed remained slim, it was no longer the impossibility it had been a short while ago.

Caitlin's battered heart swelled with hope.

Her father had once told her not only to believe in miracles but also to rely on them. If L.L. Drilling somehow warranted divine intervention, maybe it wasn't unreasonable to seek similar assistance for the blessed institution of marriage. Even one built on rocky ground and the preconceived belief that opposites attract.

Squinting against the sun, she grinned to see Donny Schaunders doing a fine imitation of a jig on a drilling floor slick with mud and oil. Her breath caught in her lungs as she realized Grant was looking straight at her. Or was that straight through her? Her heart beating in accompaniment to Donny's joyful dance, she expelled her breath in a whoosh of relief as she bent deeply at the waist and melodramatically tipped her hat to her husband.

A smile as wide as the mountain range behind him crossed Grant's face at the sight of his wife's theatrics. Considering her adamant opposition to his methods earlier in the day, he would have expected her to grudgingly attribute his success to nothing more than good luck. Having seen other marriages dissolve over such petty differences as who was right about which way the toilet paper should be unfurled on the roll, who forgot to record which check, or whose turn it was to fold socks, Caitlin never ceased to amaze him. Leave it to his sweet, charming wife to publicly acknowledge his triumph with all the grace and aplomb of an accomplished actress.

The thought of loving her for a lifetime caused his heart to thrum rapidly against his rib-cage. Taunting himself with such foolish notions was a painful endeavor. Even if it was possible that such an extraordinary woman could truly love him without regard to money, background, or a future that was uncertain at best, Grant could not bring himself to ask her to sacrifice her youth at an altar littered with men's fingers and hands, broken backs, crushed skulls, and shattered dreams. As much as he despised her for what she did to Paddy so many years ago, Laura Leigh was right after all. An oil field was not a proper place for an intelligent, beautiful young woman like Caitlin. Such a dirty, fickle business should be left to rough men who had little to offer the world but the strength of their muscles.

Even if he could somehow manage the down payment on that ranch he'd had his eye on for so long, Grant could no more ask Caitlin to trade one backbreaking job for another. He couldn't imagine her grubbing an existence from this harsh land any more than he could envision himself at a debutante ball. If she thought Wyoming's climate was severe at this time of year, how could he expect her to cope with drastic temperature changes, some of eighty degrees from one day to another in the wintertime?

With these somber thoughts in his mind, rather than blowing Caitlin a kiss from the drilling floor the way he wanted to, Grant merely turned away and got on with the business of making this hole pay out.

Caitlin refused to let her disappointment at her husband's dispassionate treatment of her to slow her down any on the job. There was a stand of pipe to be pulled, new mud to be mixed, and a myriad of other obligations to keep her busy. Knowing only too well that saving the drill bit was no guarantee of saving her father's company, she threw herself into the tasks at hand without stopping to eat. She labored beside each of the men, filling in as needed without complaint. Working herself like a machine, she tried futilely to blot out the pain caused by Grant's desire to end their marriage as soon as Paddy was strong enough to withstand the news. From the sound of the phone call she had received earlier, that day was imminent.

The single night of splendor they had shared was not enough to satisfy Caitlin for a lifetime. The memory of his hands on her body sent shivers racing through her. The recollection of how it felt to wrap him up inside her in the most intimate of acts caused an animalistic whimper to escape her lips. The thought of spending the rest of her days without the gentle man who made her complete as a woman was enough to make her feel numb to the cool breeze that stirred the dusty air around her. As the light of the day softened into a sunset that painted the horizon with rose-colored brushes, Caitlin stopped what she was doing only long enough to place her hands upon the small of her back and stretch out her aching muscles.

Unbeknownst to her Grant was watching her every move. In fact, she had never been out of his thoughts. The whole of the day he had observed her covertly, admiring her stamina and grit from a distance. Caitlin's mettle took him aback.

It seemed fate had not married him to some fainthearted damsel. Covered in layers of dust that could not mask her beauty, she looked so achingly lovely that his heart could scarce contain his emotions. Frightened to lose her, frightened to hang on to her, he was frozen to this time and spot in the universe.

Caitlin *felt* his gaze upon her as one feels the brush of angels' wings in the passing of a wispy cloud overhead. She snapped her head up in surprise, and in so doing caught him in the act of watching her with such an expression of tender devotion upon his face as to make her heart stop beating altogether. He stood a mere forty feet away from where she was positioned just outside the doghouse. It was one of the magical moments, too fragile to explain in terms mere mortals could understand, in which they regarded one another with complete and total honesty. Without a single word passing between, volumes were spoken. In the way their eyes held each other. In the way their bodies reacted to proximity uninhibited by another single soul. In the way their pulses synchronized and their blood ran hotter and faster than common sense dictated.

In that one miraculous minute there was no denying the intensity of the feelings they had for one another. The differences between them shrank beneath the heat of their mutual attraction like a drop of moisture on the lip of an erupting volcano.

Caitlin felt her knees grow wobbly beneath her own weight. A silly little smile settled on her face as she imagined the sound of bells ringing in her head. She suddenly felt dizzy.

Vaguely she wondered if some heavenly hosts weren't trying to warn her of imminent danger to her heart and soul, but before she could even finish the thought, she slumped into a heap on the floor.

Sixteen

Caitlin was not imagining the bells she heard in her head. Grant recognized the sound immediately as a death knell, the alarm signaling that they had hit a poisonous gas pocket and some had escaped from the well. Men scattered in all directions, trying to outdistance the fumes that reached out to detain them with sinister fingers. A few good whiffs of hydrogen-sulfide gas was all it took to prove fatal.

Knowing that he could either take the time to grab a gas mask and save his own life or that he could risk all odds and attempt the impossible, Grant didn't pause to consider the consequences of his actions. Glancing at the windsock on the derrick to gauge which way the breeze was blowing, he didn't so much as break stride as he ran toward the slumped figure of his wife.

The fact that he was upwind gave him all of about five seconds.

Filling his lungs with all the good air they could hold, he reached Caitlin in less than ten steps. Without giving heed to being gentle, Grant slung her over his shoulder like a sack of grain and raced to the beaver slide. Most of the crew had already shot down the frightful hundred-and-some-foot metal slide and were racing away from the site as fast as their legs would carry them.

Fighting back the tears that stung his eyes, Grant expelled the air in his lungs as slowly as was humanly possible. He didn't have the luxury of positioning himself and his cargo in the most comfortable or safe position as he hit the slide running. Pulling Caitlin into his lap, he tried to protect her as best he could while shooting through space. He hadn't risked his neck simply to break hers at the bottom of this chute straight to hell.

The air rushed past them on their perilous descent, and long tendrils of dark hair flew in his face temporarily blinding him. Holding on tight, he braced for the sudden impact of solid earth below.

They hit the catwalk with a thud that sent them careening into the dirt where they were enveloped by a cloud of dust. Choking and gasping, Grant emerged at last like some great dirty phoenix arising from the ashes of destruction. His lungs were on fire. His nostrils burned. Tears streamed down his face. Breathing hurt.

Still holding Caitlin's limp body against his chest, he lurched drunkenly toward the little trailer where an oxygen bottle was stored. By the time he reached the door, the emergency blow-out valves had done their job by clamping shut and thereby sealing the well off tight. Nonetheless the alarm bells continued ringing. The tiny bit of hydrogen sulfide that had escaped was enough to kill each and every member of the crew ten times over.

Wasting no time, Grant dropped his precious cargo upon the floor and grabbed the portable oxygen bottle and mask that he kept in the closet. He strapped the mask over his wife's pale face and feverishly checked her vital signs. Grant hadn't prayed since his parents' death, but finding himself on his knees over the prostrate body of his beloved, desperate words formed on his lips as he barraged heaven with his pleas to spare Caitlin's life.

"Please don't let her die," he implored.

Her pulse was as erratic as his own pounding heart, but Grant was reassured by the most beautiful sight in the world— his wife's chest rising and falling with each breath of cleansing oxygen that purged her lungs.

Caitlin's eyelids fluttered open. Too groggy to trust her senses, she awoke to a surreal scene: Grant kissing each of her fingers, then gently turning her hands over in his own, and pressing his lips against her open palms. The look of genuine concern, of utter devotion, etched upon his features was almost too painful to bear contemplation.

Caitlin wondered if she were lost in some sweet dream of her own making. The certainty of that fact became apparent when she brushed away the tears rolling down this big tough cowboy's face and he uttered the words that she so longed to hear.

"You can't die, Caitlin. I love you."

This must be heaven, she thought dreamily to herself. But the man who held her so tenderly in his arms was solid enough to base a future upon. And as real as the mingling of their heartbeats and their tears.

Once Grant was able to assure himself that Caitlin was truly going to be all right and that there was no need to transport her to the hospital, he carefully transferred her to the sofa. As much as he hated to leave her side, he had little choice in the matter. Duty demanded that he return to the rig, round up the crew, check on their safety, and ascertain what exactly they had hit that would cause that amount of upward pressure to close the blow-out preventers. Whatever it was, Grant knew it had to be big.

"You've got one heck of a headache coming on, darlin'," he warned. "The best thing you can do for it is to stay right here and keep on sucking on that oxygen bottle periodically.

I'll be back to check on you just as soon as I can. I want you to promise me that you won't move an inch.''

Since her throat was too raw to handle words yet, Caitlin merely nodded her head. Had she been able to speak, she would have assured her husband that she would wait an eternity for him if he would only ask her to. The sound of the front door closing behind Grant was lost to Caitlin as she entered a dream world dominated by a dark-haired giant with callused hands and gentle blue eyes which beheld her as the center of his universe.

Grant was relieved when his head count revealed all of his crew accounted for. Most had grabbed gas masks before diving from the rig like so many sailors abandoning a great ship in distress. Upon hearing the alarm signal, the others headed upwind as fast as they could force their feet to carry them. Caught unawares, Caitlin appeared to be the only one among them to have suffered any ill effects from the minute amount of poisonous gas which had escaped.

Once the alarm stopped ringing and all the instruments registered that the danger had passed, Grant hastened to return to the business of drilling for oil. His nose was twitching, and despite the disbelief such an unscientific method had evoked in his wife, he suddenly felt more hopeful than he had in weeks.

Torn between his desire to beat an unreasonable deadline and his need to be at his wife's bedside, he drove himself like a veritable slave. Between superhuman bouts of physical labor, he sneaked in peeks at Caitlin's sleeping figure. She looked so beautiful to him that he longed to take her again in his arms and smother her with kisses. Grant denied himself such selfish luxury. Covering her with an afghan, he did not disturb her sleep. When she did come to, he knew she would have a horrible, hurting headache, the intensity of which was certain to detain even someone as obstinate as his wife from attempting to go back to work until it had passed.

* * *

Caitlin awoke wondering vaguely why someone seemed so intent on kicking her head in. She couldn't remember drinking anything of an alcoholic nature that had ever packed such an ungodly wallop. Had someone slipped her a mickey?

The sight of an oxygen tank at her side brought with it the dim recollection of alarm bells. Belatedly her textbook training kicked in and the reality of what must have happened caused her to moan in agony. If merely moving her hand to her forehead caused such excruciating pain, she could only imagine what it might do to her to attempt to swing her legs over the edge of the couch and put her feet firmly on the ground.

Firmly was a relative term Caitlin realized as the room swam about her. She sat perfectly still for a long couple of minutes, cradling her head in her arms and praying that the aching which had settled into her back and all of her muscles would soon abate. Instinctively, she understood the only way to hasten that would be by getting her blood circulating. And that meant getting herself up and going, no matter how badly it was bound to hurt.

Forcing herself up on wobbly legs, Caitlin grabbed for the wall and began the slow, arduous journey to the bathroom.

Grant paled at his view of an empty sofa, a discarded afghan, and an overturned oxygen bottle. Imagining all sorts of disasters which might have befallen Caitlin, he tore through the small trailer like a madman, cursing himself all the while for not remaining at his wife's side throughout the day.

"Caitlin!" he roared in a voice made raw by panic. "Where are you?"

"In here," came a small, weak voice from another planet.

That sickly mewl led Grant to the most unlikely place he'd expected to find his ailing wife—his own bed. Caitlin's hair spilled over his pillow in a cascade of mahogany silk that took his breath away. With blankets pulled demurely up to her chin and skin so fair it was almost translucent, she reminded him of a sleeping angel.

Exquisite.

Delicate.

Precious.

"How are you feeling, baby?" he asked, gently placing his weight on the edge of the bed.

"Better," she mumbled, a soft smile playing upon her lips. "Now that you're here."

"You promised me you'd stay put," Grant chastised mildly.

Slipping a hand from beneath the covers, Caitlin smoothed out the worry lines etched upon her husband's chiseled features. "I knew I needed to get my circulation going," she explained. "That and I hoped to drown myself in the tub if the throbbing in my head didn't get any better."

Grant smiled in spite of himself. It was so like his little spitfire to crack a joke in the wake of an accident that could have well claimed her proud young life. His eyes darkened with intimate need as they swept over the lithe figure so poorly hidden beneath a single sheet and blanket. The thought of what it would be like to be met by such a sweet sight every day for the rest of his life squeezed his heart painfully in his chest.

"Just seeing you in my bed is enough to get *my* circulation going," he told her.

The warmth of his gaze was almost enough to cause Caitlin to throw off her covers. She truly was feeling better. Well enough in fact to have come to some astonishing conclusions in her short hours of confinement. Afraid that her little tussle with death may provide her husband with the impetus he'd been seeking to kick her off the rig and out of his life for good, she was determined to make her feelings known once and for all.

Grant was much like her own father, a man who would rather cut off an arm than see her hurt. Graced with more maturity and experience than she had before, Caitlin could see the truth in her mother's claim that Paddy had been so worried about her well-being on the rig that she believed removing herself from that life would ultimately save his. A man with his mind preoccupied with things other than business doesn't survive long in the oil business.

"We need to talk," Caitlin said.

Grant agreed with gentle solemnity. "Yes, we do."

Eyes the color of liquid emeralds sparkled with determination as she presented her opening arguments. "Something I thought I heard you say earlier made me deliberately seek out your bed."

Grant raised an eyebrow at the forthright nature that he had come to so respect. Her tone was so earnest he had to fight to suppress an indulgent smile.

"With every intention of making it very difficult for you to toss me out of it," she continued meeting his gaze directly.

"And just what was it I said to turn you into such a wanton vixen?" he asked in an equally solemn timbre.

Caitlin sighed in exasperation. "I was hoping you'd remember without having to be prompted," she admitted stiffly, worrying that she was sacrificing her pride on the strength of a mere dream.

"Could it be that I find you to be the most beautiful woman in the world?" Grant pondered aloud.

His words caused roses to blush in her cheeks as Caitlin shook her head no.

"Was it that you are without a doubt the finest geologist I've ever had the privilege of working with?"

Words of such high praise were gentle balm to a heart that had labored so long and hard to prove worthy, but they were not the ones Caitlin so desperately needed to hear. The lump in her throat prevented her from saying so though. Again she numbly shook her head.

Taking her chin between his thumb and forefinger, Grant gazed into eyes as soft and innocent as a child's. Such guileless eyes made him ashamed of toying with such a gentle heart for sport.

"Was it that I love you?" he asked, his voice a velvet purr. "With all of my heart? And that in the instant that you fell unconscious to the drilling floor and I thought I'd lost you, I realized how foolish I had been in rejecting the love you offered me. Is that what you thought you heard me say?"

Answering her husband with tears of joy, Caitlin most emphatically nodded her head yes.

It felt good to hear the truth spoken between them at last. Without her beside him, Grant's life lost all meaning. That which had once held monumental importance to him shrank into insignificance next to the possibility of his Caitlin's demise. A bankrupt business was nothing compared to a bankrupt heart.

Wearing the elegant gown, which she had bought with the intention of seducing him, she was to Grant the most wondrous vision his eyes had ever beheld. All satin and lace and perfumed skin as soft as angel kisses, his wife threw back her covers and beckoned him with arms outstretched.

"Come to me, my love."

It was an invitation Grant could not resist. Peeling off his clothes, he jumped into bed beside her. Burying his hands in the black cloud of her hair, he found it softer than the silken gown clinging so enticingly to her form. In contrast to the cool fabric of her negligee, Caitlin's bare shoulders were hot to his touch. Lost in the heavenly sensation of skin against skin, he groaned aloud,

When his lips brushed against hers, she opened her mouth for him and teased him unmercifully with the tip of her tongue. Driven to his limits, Grant proceeded to devour her with kisses that left her dizzy and weak and begging for more.

"See what you do to me," he commanded, taking one of her hands and guiding it to his rigid arousal.

Gripping it firmly, Caitlin tried not to gasp at the magnificence of the power entrusted to her. Fire and the desire to pleasure her husband surged through every nerve in her body. Rolling on top of him, she sought permission in eyes glittering with anticipation.

The Ice Princess of her youth melted beneath raging flames of passion. Finding herself enveloped in a conflagration beyond her control, Caitlin followed her feminine instincts in the utter trust that Grant would not intentionally hurt her. The act of mounting him was so beautiful that it brought tears to her eyes as she slid down the hard length of him. Silhouetting his heart with the fingers of both hands splayed open upon his chest, she cried out in rapture as she became one in soul and body with her husband.

Unwilling to release the woman trembling with pleasure in his arms, Grant lingered in contemplation over her irresistible face. He pushed a long, dark tendril from her cheek with his thumb. Looking deeply into eyes shimmering with love and total acceptance of who and what he was caused his voice to thicken with emotion as he put his doubts about their future into words.

"I want to renegotiate the deal we struck."

"Oh?"

Fascinated by the shape of her mouth around that single syllable, Grant drew an unsteady breath. "That's right. The terms are no longer acceptable to me. Since I agreed to them under duress I was hoping you would consider a couple of added stipulations."

"Such as?"

Caitlin quirked an inquisitive eyebrow at him. Having experienced heavenly ecstasy in his arms, she could not imagine life as anything other than Mrs. Grant Davis. Anything less would leave her without a soul.

Still, how could she possibly hold him if he was intent on getting out of their forced marriage? If he still saw her as a burden unfairly foisted upon him by a man who refused to die and relinquish his claim to a deathbed wish, Grant could be contractually bound to the last person on earth he would have chosen to have married. Knowing full well that this particular man preferred making his own decisions, Caitlin awaited the words that would affect the rest of her life.

"First off, I'd like to see that clause about this being a temporary arrangement reworded in more permanent terms," he said, fixing her with eyes that held the whole world in their depths. "Say forever."

The breath that had been trapped in her lungs came out in a whoosh of relief as she threw her arms around his neck.

"Forever sounds good to me," she sobbed, almost strangling on the joy which clogged her throat.

Grant stroked her hair lovingly for a long moment before speaking again. When he did at last, his voice too cracked with emotion. "I hope you know that I have nothing to offer you but my love."

The shattering tenderness of that admission stirred her soul. He truly loved her! Despite his worries to the contrary, Caitlin was quite sure that she could live on nothing but the nectar of those words until the very end of time.

"It's more than enough."

"Not for your mother," he mumbled, watching twilight cast its purple cloak over the lengthening shadows of the day.

Cuddling against the full length of his naked body, Caitlin commanded his full attention. "You just leave Mother to me and concentrate on making *us* happy."

Seventeen

"**H**ave I ever mentioned how much I like that nightie?" Grant asked his wife over a steaming cup of coffee.

Wiggling her eyebrows, Caitlin made a self-deprecating little moue as she twirled around full circle. "You mean this old thing?"

Playfulness added just the right spice to a breakfast of bacon, eggs, and cinnamon toast. The scent of commitment complimented the delicious smell wafting through the small trailer. Though hope of financial security lay dormant beneath layers of stubborn earth, Grant and Caitlin had discovered something far more precious in each other's arms.

Last night between bouts of heavenly passion, they had shared with each other their hopes and dreams, awakening in the morning with the understanding that love supersedes mere lust and defies rational thought. While most couples discuss the intimate details of their expectations before marriage, they were still negotiating uncharted territory. For instance, Grant was first surprised then delighted to discover that although her career was important to Caitlin, she had no desire whatsoever to postpone having babies.

His babies.

Lots of them. So they would never have to be as lonely as they both had been growing up as only children. They agreed that siblings would add a dimension of insight and an added layer of support to help one another through tough times.

Grant had never allowed himself to think of raising a family with such an incredible woman. That a lifetime plagued by loneliness would be soon filled with the sound of laughter and the patter of miniature versions of the two of them was nothing short of miraculous to him. In between kisses, he promised Caitlin however many children she wanted—just so long as each and every one was the product of their love.

Filled with a sense of utter well-being, Grant felt the need to share his joy with the man who had made it all possible. "What do we say we take the afternoon off and drive into Casper to see your father?"

Caitlin's face broke into a radiant smile. "You know how much that would mean to him—and to me! Talking to him on the phone every day just isn't the same as seeing him in person."

Grant knew only that he was willing to spend every day for the rest of his life working to keep that smile affixed to his lovely wife's face. Gazing across the table at her, he felt as if he were seeing an angel materialize before his eyes. "You are so beautiful," he observed. "How *did* I ever get so lucky?"

"I believe you were coerced into it," Caitlin replied with complete candor. "Still if you're able to dole out compliments this early in the day before I even get a chance to run a brush through my hair, you must really be committed to making this crazy marriage work."

"You better believe I am. Come here," he invited smoothly, his eyes darkening with a craving for something other than food.

Caitlin needed no further prompting. Setting her own cup of coffee down, she obediently positioned herself in her husband's lap. His lips found hers a willing accomplice. He kissed her with such expertise that she was left breathless at the end of it. Breathless and eager for more.

No less than a lifetime more.

That their food grew cold was no fault of the heat generated by their early morning passion. Grateful that her husband was wearing nothing more than a pair of formfitting, worn jeans, Caitlin ran her hands over his bare chest. "I can't get enough of touching you," she confessed in a whisper.

Opening her robe to his gaze and roaming hands, Grant admitted the same. Satiated from a night of incredible love-making, he was amazed that the mere sight of his wife's breasts demurely covered by strategically placed satin appliqués was enough to arouse him to the point of dragging her back to bed without further sustenance.

A loud knock at the front door made him groan aloud. The intrusion merely confirmed the obvious. This was one meal destined to be eaten cold.

Not eager for any of the crew to see his wife in such a lovely state of disarray, Grant rose reluctantly to his feet. "I'll get it," he said, giving her a sexually scorching look that said *don't move a muscle; I'll be right back.*

Irritated by the insistence of the intruder pounding upon his door, he pasted a threatening scowl upon his face and padded barefoot across the room.

"This had better be important," he muttered under his breath. Throwing the door wide-open, he barked, "What is it *now?*"

His mother- and father-in-law stood on the other side of the open doorway, wearing matching startled expressions at the obvious lack of hospitality with which they were greeted. Laura Leigh jumped as the door swung open. Had Paddy not held her at the elbow, it appeared she might have fled.

Grant gaped at them in disbelief. "What are you doing here?" he stammered.

"Aren't you going to invite us in?" countered a smooth,

cultured voice tinged with reproach at the idea that they might just be left standing on the stoop indefinitely.

Immediately recognizing that voice as belonging to her mother, Caitlin vaulted across the room without regard to her state of dishevelment. The sight of her father standing next to Laura Leigh was so unexpected that it stopped her in midstride.

"Daddy!" she squealed as both parents stepped inside the trailer.

The next thing Caitlin knew she was being enveloped in the first family hug that she could remember in years. Belatedly she remembered that the newest addition to that fragile family unit had been unintentionally left out of their circle of love. Slipping an arm around Grant's waist, she attempted to draw him in, only to feel resistance in his tense muscles. The one at his jaw throbbed with tension.

Closing the door behind them, Caitlin attempted to put everyone at ease. "What are you doing up and out of bed?" she asked her father in a tone that vacillated between respect and a scolding.

Mussed, her hair formed a dark, lovely cloud about a face flushed with passion. Her robe gaped open, revealing far more about what was going on in her marriage than she was ready to discuss at the moment.

Her mother and father looked at one another in uncomfortable silence. The knowing look they shared put a toothy grin on Paddy's face. Laura Leigh's lips tightened into a tight pucker. Self-consciously Caitlin tugged her robe shut but was unable to cover the telltale blush that crept from beneath its neckline.

Remembering both her manners and her father's condition, she invited them to "Come on in and sit down."

"Your mother was worried that I'd made a mistake forcing you two together, but it looks like you kids are getting along just fine," Paddy ventured awkwardly, searching his daughter's green eyes for assurance. "If you wouldn't mind putting her mind at ease, we'll get out of your hair and let you get back to whatever you were doing.''

The dark look Laura Leigh shot him wiped the hopeful smile from his face. Pale and contrite, he shrugged his shoulders. Caitlin rushed to help him to the couch.

''I never expected you to get out of the hospital so soon,'' she admitted. ''How are you feeling? What did the doctors tell you? What kind of medicine do they have you on? What about physical therapy? Have you started an exercise program?''

Paddy did his best to dodge the questions that came at him like bullets. Holding up his hands in surrender as he took his seat, he begged her to slow down and take a breath. ''Whoa there, little girl. One thing at a time, please.''

Stepping over to the couch, Grant extended Paddy his hand. ''It's good to see you,'' he said in a voice kept deliberately even so as not to expose the onslaught of emotions threatening to come to the surface.

Paddy's handshake was considerably weaker than Grant had remembered it, but the warmth in the older man's eyes hadn't dimmed at all. ''It's good to see you too, Grant,'' he replied. ''Damn good.''

They had barely unclasped hands when Laura Leigh announced in a crisp regal voice, ''Caitlin dear, your father has something to tell you.''

Her tone suggested that the news they were about to hear was not good. In fact, Paddy's manner implied that had it not been for Laura Leigh's presence he would have avoided the subject altogether. Squirming uncomfortably, he looked like a recalcitrant child who had just been hauled into the principal's office for high crimes on the playground.

''Paddy!'' Laura Leigh prodded. ''You promised to…''

''Can't you see with your own two eyes how unnecessary it is?''

As resolute as the statue of justice, Laura Leigh would have none of his excuses. Grant had never seen anybody back Paddy down as this lady did with nothing more than a determined glint in eyes just a shade lighter than her daughter's.

"What is it?"

Caitlin took a seat beside her father and steeled herself against the possibility that the doctors had discovered something horrible during his recovery period in the hospital. Taking his hand, she held it prayerfully in both of hers. Surely God would not be so cruel as to strike her father down now that she had found perfect happiness as Grant's wife. Now that she was ready to provide Paddy with that passel of grandchildren he had always wanted.

The reassuring squeeze her father exerted upon her hand was in complete contradiction to the anxious look upon his face.

"If it's about the rig," Grant interjected. "You have to know that we did the very best we could. Even so, I feel I've let you down. I've got to be honest with you. I doubt if we're going to make it."

The smile upon Paddy's face surprised both Grant and Caitlin.

"I have a whole new outlook on what's important and what's not. Businesses come and go. Family is forever."

Grant was puzzled by the look he exchanged with Laura Leigh. Had he only imagined the intimacy in that gaze? More than likely it was simply Paddy's way of reining in Laura Leigh's anger at discovering that the marriage of convenience he had arranged for their daughter had developed into something much more real. And far more physical than what she had been led to believe when they had left her back at the hospital in Casper.

Pride would not allow Grant to hang his head. If Laura Leigh was expecting an apology from him, she would be standing there a long, long time. He wasn't about to apologize for falling in love with her daughter.

Unable to stand the suspense any longer, Caitlin asked, "What is it you want to tell us, Daddy?"

"If you won't tell them, I will," Laura Leigh said, shaking a reproving finger at Paddy.

"Can't you please just let it be?" he implored.

"Marriage shouldn't be based upon falsehood, and I've already told you that I'll have no part of it," she told him. Turning her attention to the young people in the room, she continued as smoothly as if she were merely pressing a wrinkle from her immaculate cream-colored pants. "Caitlin, I think you have the right to know that although your father was seriously ill in the hospital, he deliberately played it up some in hopes of manipulating you into marrying the man he had hand-picked for you."

Caitlin looked at Grant.

Grant looked at Caitlin.

They provided one another a perfect mirror of their utter incredulity. Laura Leigh might as well have told them she was running off to join the circus as to have made such a preposterous claim.

"I know it was wrong of me, but you have to know that it was your happiness I was thinking of. Why, anybody could see that you two were meant for one another." The little catch in Paddy's voice exposed the truth of Laura Leigh's allegations.

"Anybody but us, apparently?" Caitlin asked numbly. The fact that her father could be so conniving was taking time to sink in.

Sheepishly Paddy nodded his head. "You two were mighty pigheaded when it came to seeing what was right before your eyes. You have to believe that I was acting in your best interest. And for a while there, the doctors really *did* think I was a goner. Is it so much to ask to wish for grandchildren at my age? And what beautiful children they would surely be. And smart of course," he added in a hopeful tone.

The young couple before him was shaking their heads in disbelief at what they were hearing. Nobody likes to be manipulated. Certainly no one as headstrong as either Grant or Caitlin.

At that particular moment, nothing could have moved either one to admit to the old codger that he'd been right. A tacit agreement was reached in the look that they exchanged. Paddy deserved to sweat it out before being forgiven.

After a tangibly uncomfortable amount of time had passed, Laura Leigh pulled an official-looking paper from her purse. She unfolded it and passed it to Grant.

"It's your annulment papers," she said as calmly as if she were handing him a particularly interesting article in the local paper. "I gather by both of your reactions that you're still as anxious to sign this as you led me to believe last time we spoke."

Grant responded like a rattlesnake that had its tail stepped on. "I suppose this has nothing whatsoever to do with the way you feel about marrying your debutante daughter off to some lowly oil field hand?"

"As a matter of fact, it doesn't."

He couldn't believe how cool and indifferent to his anger Laura Leigh was. His mother-in-law had the blood of an IRS agent running in her veins. "Look, lady. There's no way you can make me feel guilty for falling in love with your daughter. Or make me feel like I'm not good enough for her."

Laura Leigh arched an aristocratic eyebrow at this startling admission.

"Am I to understand that you have changed your mind then?"

Grant looked at her in shock. "Has it ever occurred to you that your daughter is made of sterner stuff than you? That maybe, unlike you, she won't up and leave me at the first sign of trouble? That she's not ashamed to be married to a poor oil field cowboy. That just because you don't personally approve of me, you have no right to—"

"Back off, son."

The sound of Paddy's voice filled the room with the strength of its command. Fire flashed in his old Irish eyes as he stood up and addressed Grant man to man.

"I don't like the tone you're taking with my wife."

Grant and Caitlin's mouths dropped open at the same time as Laura Leigh flashed a wedding ring in their startled faces.

Caitlin recognized it as the same one Paddy had given her so many years ago. Her mother had kept it secreted away in her jewelry box since the time they had separated.

"I never had the heart to give it up," Laura Leigh admitted to her daughter. "For some silly sentimental reason I brought it along with me when I caught the plane to Wyoming."

"Good thing you did," Paddy interrupted, snaking an arm protectively around her waist. "It came in handy when the priest who performed the ceremony for you two assisted us in renewing our vows. You see, all these years neither one of us could ever bring ourselves to actually file for divorce."

Paddy's explanation that old feelings were rekindled in the hospital and a long overdue reconciliation was reached seemed too much for Grant to comprehend. He stood woodenly off to the side as Caitlin launched herself into her mother's arms first, then her father's. Clearly she was beyond delighted at the unexpected turn of events.

Grant wished he could share her enthusiasm. He'd already gotten off on the wrong foot with the mother-in-law whom he'd mistakenly believed would have little more impact on his life than a brief annual visit to see the grandkids. If she and Paddy really were back together for good, this barracuda would undoubtedly be a more constant presence than he'd anticipated. The thought of battling his in-laws on a daily basis was not something he relished.

Abruptly Laura Leigh turned to him and asked point-blank. "Whatever gave you the idea that I don't like you?"

Caught off guard, he stammered, "I just assumed that because you left Paddy and went back to your life as a socialite that you wouldn't much care to see your daughter married off to a man who doesn't have much more than a couple of dimes to rub together. I assumed you'd think that—"

"That she's too good for you?"

When Grant nodded his head in assent, Laura Leigh confirmed his suspicions. The woman was nothing if not brutally honest.

"She is. But then I'm going to think my baby is too good

for any man. That's my prerogative as her mother. I just hope you know how lucky you are. She'll be a wonderful wife. Admittedly a better one than I made Paddy, but there's still time for me to make up for my mistakes, and I have a good teacher. Caitlin can give us all some invaluable lessons in love.''

Moved to tears by her mother's words, Caitlin wrapped an arm around Grant. Gently she nudged him to take the first step toward establishing family harmony.

''All I expect of you, Grant,'' Laura Leigh continued. ''All either of us expects is that you take good care of our little girl. I never have based my opinion of a man on how much money he has in his bank account. I prefer to save the judgment for how much love he has in his heart.''

His mother-in-law's eloquence astounded Grant. All this time he'd been thinking of this woman as a praying mantis, devouring the bodies of her male victims, and come to find out, she was a fine lady indeed. Once he got to know her even better, he suspected that they just might become good friends. When she held out her arms to him, he didn't hesitate to walk into her embrace.

She smelled of honeysuckle, of old money, and fresh beginnings.

When Grant started to apologize, Laura Leigh silenced him with a wave of her hand. ''What are you two planning on doing now that the company is defunct as I understand it?''

It was a fair question. One uttered out of genuine concern rather than as an accusation. Grant knew his humble dream of owning a ranch was little in comparison to what Caitlin could have so easily married into. A lump of embarrassment stuck in his throat.

His wife didn't give him a chance to try to dislodge it as she launched into a description of the place Grant had his heart set on buying. She spoke with all the enthusiasm of an experienced salesman. Strangely enough the more she talked, the less preposterous it sounded. Caitlin insisted that she didn't care where they lived. For the rest of her life, home would be wherever Grant was.

"I don't care if he wants to raise goats, pigs, or potatoes in Hawaii. Just so long as he wants me at his side," Caitlin assured everyone in the room, including her husband, who needed to hear it most of all.

Taking her in his arms, Grant held his bride against a heart brimming with joy. In the shadow of financial ruin, he had never been happier in his life. The cold past was to be banished from his heart forever as together they embarked on a new life filled with love and hope and trust.

While Caitlin searched the cupboards for four glasses, Grant popped the cork on a bottle of champagne. Though he had been saving it for the day they hit oil, he could think of no better time to celebrate than the present.

That they were broke was suddenly of little consequence. Never was there a more jubilant crew than the foursome toasting one another around a small kitchenette table that could barely accommodate them all.

"To love," Grant proposed, ripping the annulment papers in half and tossing them in the air.

"To love," they all exclaimed to the clinking of cheap plastic glasses.

As they all drank deeply of their shared loving cups, Caitlin became aware that something was amiss. It took her a long moment of introspection to figure out that it was in fact the silence that was so out of place. Deafening in its totality, it engulfed her senses.

"Listen," she said, cocking her head toward the rig.

To an untrained ear the normal daily noise level on a drilling rig can be overwhelming in its intensity. The reverberation of the variety of sounds carries for rig workers important information that could save their lives and assures bosses that business is under way as it should be. That no noise at all reached Caitlin's ears was definite cause for concern. Though she couldn't blame them if they had, she couldn't quite bring herself to believe that the crew had given up before the actual last day of the deadline that had been looming over their heads like ominous thunderclouds.

"Do you hear it?" she asked the people huddled about the small kitchenette table.

A sudden rumbling deep beneath the trailer made her think of some great slumbering monster being awakened by the grumbling of its own empty belly. Caitlin set her glass down and watched it shiver on the tabletop.

"What's happening? Is it an earthquake?" she asked, grabbing the only pair of shoulders she knew to be broad enough to bear the entire weight of the world.

"No, honey. Something much, much better," Grant exclaimed. He placed a reassuring kiss on the top of her head as he raced to the window.

Paddy beat him there. "Come look!" he hollered.

What was obvious to both her husband and father was made clear to Caitlin only when she peered out behind the curtains herself. She spied the entire crew high above them on the drilling floor, whooping and howling and dancing about as if they had just drained a vat of hard cider. The impact of their revelry dawned slowly upon her. The reason the rig was quiet was that the emergency pressure valves had shut off the well, stopping the crude oil from shooting out of the top of the rig as in days of old. The rumbling they heard was caused by the intense amount of pressure trying to force its way to the surface.

"We've struck oil!" she squeaked.

Hitting bottom hole on schedule meant L.L. Drilling was going to be solvent for some time to come. And the bonus it meant for Grant would enable him to put a down payment on the ranch of his dreams. A place where he and Caitlin could spend a lifetime learning to know one another better. A place where they could concentrate on raising a family and appreciating the abundance of the land. A place where they could face life's challenges on their own terms—together.

Grant lifted Caitlin up in his arms and twirled her around and around the small living room. Dizzy with joy, laughter mingled with kisses as Paddy proceeded to pour everyone another drink. Surrounded by the people he loved most in the world, the man who had spent a lifetime banking on miracles hoisted his glass in the air and made yet another toast.

"To Love's fair sisters, Tenacity and Luck!"

* * * * *

Please watch for another provocative
love story in the theme promotion
THE BRIDAL BID *with*

MARRIAGE FOR SALE
by
Carol Devine

On sale in February 2000,
only in Silhouette Desire!

If you enjoyed what you just read,
then we've got an offer you can't resist!

Take 2 bestselling love stories FREE!

Plus get a FREE surprise gift!

January 2000
HER FOREVER MAN
#1267 by Leanne Banks
Lone Star Families: The Logans

February 2000
A BRIDE FOR JACKSON POWERS
#1273 by Dixie Browning
The Passionate Powers

March 2000
A COWBOY'S SECRET
#1279 by Anne McAllister
Code of the West

April 2000
LAST DANCE
#1285 by Cait London
Freedom Valley

May 2000
DR. IRRESISTIBLE
#1291 by Elizabeth Bevarly
From Here to Maternity

June 2000
TOUGH TO TAME
#1297 by Jackie Merritt

MAN OF THE MONTH

For twenty years Silhouette has been giving you
the ultimate in romantic reads. Come join the
celebration as some of your favorite authors
help celebrate our anniversary with the most
sensual, emotional love stories ever!

Available at your favorite retail outlet.

Silhouette®

Where love comes alive™

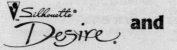 **and**

bring you

The Passionate Powers—men bound by blood, tied to the sea and destined to be heroes.

Meet the Powers men:

Jackson Powers in
A BRIDE FOR JACKSON POWERS
by Dixie Browning,
a February 2000 Silhouette Desire title.

Matthew Powers in
THE PAPER MARRIAGE
by Bronwyn Williams,
an August 2000 Harlequin Historicals title.

Curt Powers in
THE VIRGIN AND THE VENGEFUL GROOM
by Dixie Browning,
a November 2000 Silhouette Desire title.

Don't miss this exciting new series from
Silhouette Desire and Harlequin Historicals!

Available at your favorite retail outlet.

SILHOUETTE'S 20TH ANNIVERSARY CONTEST
OFFICIAL RULES
NO PURCHASE NECESSARY TO ENTER

1. To enter, follow directions published in the offer to which you are responding. Contest begins 1/1/00 and ends on 8/24/00 (the "Promotion Period"). Method of entry may vary. Mailed entries must be postmarked by 8/24/00, and received by 8/31/00.

2. During the Promotion Period, the Contest may be presented via the Internet. Entry via the Internet may be restricted to residents of certain geographic areas that are disclosed on the Web site. To enter via the Internet, if you are a resident of a geographic area in which Internet entry is permissible, follow the directions displayed on-line, including typing your essay of 100 words or fewer telling us "Where In The World Your Love Will Come Alive." On-line entries must be received by 11:59 p.m. Eastern Standard time on 8/24/00. Limit one e-mail entry per person, household and e-mail address per day, per presentation. If you are a resident of a geographic area in which entry via the Internet is permissible, you may, in lieu of submitting an entry on-line, enter by mail, by hand-printing your name, address, telephone number and contest number/name on an 8"x 11" plain piece of paper and telling us in 100 words or fewer "Where In The World Your Love Will Come Alive," and mailing via first-class mail to: Silhouette 20th Anniversary Contest, (in the U.S.) P.O. Box 9069, Buffalo, NY 14269-9069; (In Canada) P.O. Box 637, Fort Erie, Ontario, Canada L2A 5X3. Limit one 8"x 11" mailed entry per person, household and e-mail address per day. On-line and/or 8"x 11" mailed entries received from persons residing in geographic areas in which Internet entry is not permissible will be disqualified. No liability is assumed for lost, late, incomplete, inaccurate, nondelivered or misdirected mail, or misdirected e-mail, for technical, hardware or software failures of any kind, lost or unavailable network connection, or failed, incomplete, garbled or delayed computer transmission or any human error which may occur in the receipt or processing of the entries in the contest.

3. Essays will be judged by a panel of members of the Silhouette editorial and marketing staff based on the following criteria:

   Sincerity (believability, credibility)—50%

   Originality (freshness, creativity)—30%

   Aptness (appropriateness to contest ideas)—20%

   Purchase or acceptance of a product offer does not improve your chances of winning. In the event of a tie, duplicate prizes will be awarded.

4. All entries become the property of Harlequin Enterprises Ltd., and will not be returned. Winner will be determined no later than 10/31/00 and will be notified by mail. Grand Prize winner will be required to sign and return Affidavit of Eligibility within 15 days of receipt of notification. Noncompliance within the time period may result in disqualification and an alternative winner may be selected. All municipal, provincial, federal, state and local laws and regulations apply. Contest open only to residents of the U.S. and Canada who are 18 years of age or older, and is void wherever prohibited by law. Internet entry is restricted solely to residents of those geographical areas in which Internet entry is permissible. Employees of Torstar Corp., their affiliates, agents and members of their immediate families are not eligible. Taxes on the prizes are the sole responsibility of winners. Entry and acceptance of any prize offered constitutes permission to use winner's name, photograph or other likeness for the purposes of advertising, trade and promotion on behalf of Torstar Corp. without further compensation to the winner, unless prohibited by law. Torstar Corp and D.L. Blair, Inc., their parents, affiliates and subsidiaries, are not responsible for errors in printing or electronic presentation of contest or entries. In the event of printing or other errors which may result in unintended prize values or duplication of prizes, all affected contest materials or entries shall be null and void. If for any reason the Internet portion of the contest is not capable of running as planned, including infection by computer virus, bugs, tampering, unauthorized intervention, fraud, technical failures, or any other causes beyond the control of Torstar Corp. which corrupt or affect the administration, secrecy, fairness, integrity or proper conduct of the contest, Torstar Corp. reserves the right, at its sole discretion, to disqualify any individual who tampers with the entry process and to cancel, terminate, modify or suspend the contest or the Internet portion thereof. In the event of a dispute regarding an on-line entry, the entry will be deemed submitted by the authorized holder of the e-mail account submitted at the time of entry. Authorized account holder is defined as the natural person who is assigned to an e-mail address by an Internet access provider, on-line service provider or other organization that is responsible for arranging e-mail address for the domain associated with the submitted e-mail address.

5. Prizes: Grand Prize—a $10,000 vacation to anywhere in the world. Travelers (at least one must be 18 years of age or older) or parent or guardian if one traveler is a minor, must sign and return a Release of Liability prior to departure. Travel must be completed by December 31, 2001, and is subject to space and accommodations availability. Two hundred (200) Second Prizes—a two-book limited edition autographed collector set from one of the Silhouette Anniversary authors: Nora Roberts, Diana Palmer, Linda Howard or Annette Broadrick (value $10.00 each set). All prizes are valued in U.S. dollars.

6. For a list of winners (available after 10/31/00), send a self-addressed, stamped envelope to: Harlequin Silhouette 20th Anniversary Winners, P.O. Box 4200, Blair, NE 68009-4200.

Contest sponsored by Torstar Corp., P.O. Box 9042, Buffalo, NY 14269-9042.

ENTER FOR
A CHANCE TO WIN*

Silhouette's 20th Anniversary Contest

Tell Us Where in the World
You Would Like *Your* Love To Come Alive...
And We'll Send the Lucky Winner There!

Silhouette wants to take you wherever
your happy ending can come true.

Here's how to enter: Tell us, in 100 words or less,
where you want to go to make your love come alive!

In addition to the grand prize, there will be 200
runner-up prizes, collector's-edition book sets
autographed by one of the Silhouette anniversary
authors: **Nora Roberts, Diana Palmer,
Linda Howard** or **Annette Broadrick**.

DON'T MISS YOUR CHANCE TO WIN!
ENTER NOW! No Purchase Necessary

Where love comes alive™

Name: _____

Address: _____

City: _____ State/Province: _____

Zip/Postal Code: _____

Mail to Harlequin Books: **In the U.S.**: P.O. Box 9069, Buffalo, NY
14269-9069; **In Canada**: P.O. Box 637, Fort Erie, Ontario, L4A 5X3

*No purchase necessary—for contest details send a self-addressed stamped envelope to:
Silhouette's 20th Anniversary Contest, P.O. Box 9069, Buffalo, NY, 14269-9069 (include
contest name on self-addressed envelope). Residents of Washington and Vermont may
omit postage. Open to Cdn. (excluding Quebec) and U.S. residents who are 18 or over.
Void where prohibited. Contest ends August 31, 2000.

PS20CON_R